R0701961674   11/2023

PALM BEACH COUNTY
LIBRARY SYSTEM
3650 Summit Boulevard
West Palm Beach, FL   33406-4198

Stuck With You

D1606438

Stuck With You

'NATHAN BURGOINE

JAMES LORIMER & COMPANY LTD., PUBLISHERS
TORONTO

Copyright © 2023 by 'Nathan Burgoine

All rights reserved. No part of this book may be reproduced or transmitted in any form or by any means, electronic or mechanical, including photocopying, or by any information storage or retrieval system, without permission in writing from the publisher.

James Lorimer & Company Ltd., Publishers acknowledges funding support from the Ontario Arts Council (OAC), an agency of the Government of Ontario. We acknowledge the support of the Canada Council for the Arts, which last year invested $153 million to bring the arts to Canadians throughout the country. This project has been made possible in part by the Government of Canada and with the support of Ontario Creates.

Cover design: Tyler Cleroux
Cover illustration: Jordan Masciarelli

Library and Archives Canada Cataloguing in Publication

Title: Stuck with you / 'Nathan Burgoine.
Names: Burgoine, 'Nathan, author.
Identifiers: Canadiana 20220485119 | ISBN 9781459417205 (softcover) | ISBN 9781459417274 (hardcover) | 9781459417427 (epub)
Subjects: LCGFT: Novels.
Classification: LCC PS8603.U73713 S78 2023 | DDC jC813/.6—dc23

Published by:
James Lorimer &
Company Ltd., Publishers
117 Peter Street, Suite 304
Toronto, ON, Canada
M5V 0M3
www.lorimer.ca

Distributed in Canada by:
Formac Lorimer Books
5502 Atlantic Street
Halifax, NS, Canada
B3H 1G4
www.formaclorimerbooks.ca

Distributed in the US by:
Lerner Publisher Services
241 1st Ave. N.
Minneapolis, MN, USA
55401
www.lernerbooks.com

Printed and bound in Canada
Manufactured by Friesens Corporation in Altona, Manitoba, Canada in February 2023.
Job #295017

This book is for all the young queer kids
who don't have an answer for
"What do you want to be when you grow up?"
Me neither.

01 Caleb Khoury Ruins Everything

I USUALLY LIKE taking the train. I don't even mind Toronto Union Station. It's a maze that seems to always be under construction, but I've been here a lot. I know my way around and I like it when I know where I'm going. Which I guess is also why I like trains. My best friend, Raj, says my comfort zones are all about not having to worry about surprises. I don't think they mean it as an insult, and I don't take it as one. It's true. I like knowing what's going to happen. I read spoilers before I watch movies. Once I find something I like at a restaurant, I order it every time.

So when I'm in Union Station? I'm usually in a good mood when I'm waiting for my train. Or I'm in a better mood, anyway. I usually look forward to having four and a half hours to come down from a week in Toronto with my father. I don't hate Toronto or anything, but I didn't grow up here. My three weeks a year are more than enough. There's only so much fun I can have watching my father look like he'd rather be working, or listening while he talks at me about what I'm going to do after school.

Not *to* me. *At* me. There's a difference.

My father thinks if he tells me enough times I should know what I want to do for the rest of my life that somehow I'll just pick something. He thinks I could do accounting, like him. Or teaching, like my mother. He doesn't get that I barely managed to get a B in my math classes. I'm pretty sure accountants need to do math. And the idea of going to school for the rest of my life, even as the teacher?

So much no.

Normally, though, I wouldn't be sitting here thinking about all the stuff my dad didn't understand. Usually, at this point, I'd have my earbuds in and be listening to whatever playlist Raj has sent my way, and already feeling the nine days with my father wearing off. I'd text Raj what I thought of each song as I listened. They make the *best* playlists. And before I knew it, it would be time to board, and I'd be on my way home to Ottawa.

Back to my friends. Back to my mom and my stepdad and my sisters. Back where I have a bedroom, not a pull-out couch in my father's office. Back to where I belonged.

Unfortunately, this year was different. This year, I was sitting on the bench in Union Station without my earbuds, because my phone was in my backpack with a completely shattered screen. I had no way to listen to music, no way to text Raj or any of my other friends in the Rainbow Club, all thanks to Caleb Khoury's damn basketball.

It had been the same on the ride up to Toronto, only worse. Because on the way here, those nine days with my father were still ahead of me, and the loss of my phone had been so fresh.

Ugh.

Whatever. Raj would tell me I needed to lose this mood. The week with my father was over. Soon they'd call for boarding, and I'd be on my way home. I could sketch on the train, even if everything would turn out a little bumpy. Also, this was the last March Break of my life. I never had to do this again.

There. I'd found a positive mood. Raj would be proud. They'd have offered me a fist bump. They were all about finding positive moods.

Thinking of Raj made me think of Prom and how our plans for everyone in the Rainbow Club to head to Prom as a big friend group had gotten *complicated*. Lin and Jasmine's breakup at the end of February had been unexpected.

Jasmine dating Roy less than a week later?

That had been huge. Lin was hurt to be so quickly

replaced. Grayson had said Jasmine shouldn't come with us to Prom anymore, and everything was a mess now. I hated that the group seemed to have decided picking sides was so important, when as far as I could tell this wasn't about sides. It took a week or two, but Lin admitted she and Jasmine weren't right for each other. Lin wasn't holding any sort of grudge. But half the club seem to have decided Jasmine didn't belong anymore. And when I tried to talk to Grayson about it, he'd gotten mad.

I backed down like I always did. I'd told myself I'd text everyone over March Break. I figured between Raj and me, we'd figure something out.

Except, thanks to Caleb Khoury, I couldn't text anyone. I couldn't find out what was happening. I couldn't try to fix anything.

Fixing things was my other comfort zone, Raj said. I didn't like it when people were upset. If there was something I could do to make my friends happy, I'd do it.

But instead, I'd been pretty much cut off for nine days and it felt like forever. I'd had to resort to email and direct messages on my father's computer whenever he wasn't working or telling me I needed to have a plan for after high school. Which wasn't often.

I hadn't told my father about my plan to take a gap year. I knew he wouldn't like it.

My positive mood crashed and burned.

They announced the first boarding for my train, and I pulled the printed page out of my hoodie pocket, complete with the QR code I'd normally show them on my phone. I walked to the front and the little scanner thing the guy in the vest used didn't work the first two times he tried. The third time it finally pinged, and I made my way up the escalator, and then along the tracks where my train waited for me. My train car was pretty close to the front, so I carried my bag and my backpack and made my way.

Ahead of me, a guy in a suit was already on his phone, talking. I couldn't imagine being on a train in a suit. I'm definitely happier in my hoodie and jeans. It's four and a half hours, and I'm going to wear something comfortable.

Also, it's not like I have a suit. Although I really needed to figure out what I'm going to wear to Prom.

Assuming we were all still going to Prom.

Man, I wished I could text Raj. I was sure they already knew what they were planning to wear. I wanted to text Lin, too. I wanted to check in with her and see if she was feeling any better. I bet she'd also have her outfit picked out.

I found my seat about two-thirds of the way down the car and took a few seconds to put my coat and bag in the overhead compartment. I slid my backpack into the space under the seat in front of me, so I'd have my stuff at hand. I had the window seat, which was nice. By the time I sat down, I could feel Toronto already getting left behind, even though the train hadn't started moving yet.

There. I'd found a positive mood again. I gave Raj another imaginary fist bump.

I watched the people boarding while I waited for the train car to fill up. Mostly older people, about half in couples, and only a few kids. No one took the seat beside me. As more and more people climbed on board, I was starting to think I won the train lottery. Having an empty seat beside me would be awesome, especially since I didn't have a way to tune out any noise. On the ride up, the man beside me had spent the whole trip using his laptop, typing up a report or presentation or something. He'd worn earbuds, which meant he didn't have to listen to his own tap-tap-tap, but I did.

I waited, and waited, and no one else seemed to be coming onto our train car. Was I going to have an empty seat? From the looks of things, it was only one of two empty seats left on the whole train car.

This was great.

Then one more person climbed aboard. He had a black hoodie on, hood up, and grey sweatpants. He walked right past the first empty seat. Damn. He'd be sitting with me, then. He wasn't in a suit at least, which might mean no typing. The guy kept coming down the aisle and I stared.

Oh no. Oh *please* no.

I knew that face. I knew the chin with the dent in

it. And I knew the black hair cut pretty short and yet still just a bit messy. I knew the dark brown eyes and the big smile. The *annoyingly* cute smile. Beneath the loose black hoodie, I happened to know he was stocky and had nice arms. All the better to throw a basketball.

I barely stopped myself from swearing out loud.

The guy in the black hoodie?

Caleb freaking Khoury.

This couldn't be happening. This had to be a joke.

But it wasn't a joke. Caleb walked all the way down the aisle looking at the little numbers printed above the seats and stopped right beside me, his duffel bag in his hands. He blinked when he saw me.

"Oh," he said. He smiled, even. "Hey, Ben."

I glared at him. *Really*? After the last nine days, after *everything* he did, all he was going to do was smile and say "Hey, Ben"?

Caleb's smile faded when I didn't answer, and he opened the compartment to put his duffel away. If anything, he seemed a little confused. But mostly he didn't seem to care.

Typical.

Okay. I needed a plan. If I was going to have Caleb Khoury beside me for the next four and a half hours, I'd lose my mind.

The only plan I could think of was to ignore him. I'd pretend he didn't exist.

He had a backpack on as well, which he pulled off and put under the seat in front of him. He closed the compartment and sat down beside me, tugging his hood down and turning to face me. His hair was doing the messy-but-cool thing. I had to use so much hair gel to make my hair look even close to that good.

So annoying.

"You okay, man?" Caleb flashed another one of his smiles.

That was it. I'd spent the last ten days cut off from my friends while my entire friend group fell apart, listening to my father list all the things I was doing wrong, and now I was going to have to sit beside the guy who'd made my March Break suck even worse? Every plan I had to ignore him went right out the window. He was acting like nothing happened. Good hair or not, Caleb Khoury was a complete and utter *asshole*.

"Are you kidding me?" I snapped. "Of course, I'm not okay. *Man*."

02 Caleb Khoury Sucks at Apologies

CALEB FROWNED. He had a little line between his eyebrows, and he sort of tilted his head at me like a puppy when it hears a strange sound.

"What's wrong?" he said.

"Seriously?" I said. He could *not* be this clueless, could he?

He did another head tilt and lifted both hands into the air. Not in surrender, more like a "Woah there!" way. After a second, though, he stopped frowning and started smiling. Now he didn't look confused, he looked amused. "Wait. Are you mad about the basketball?"

He said it like if I was still mad, it would be the most ridiculous thing in the world. Why had I even said anything? I should have put my earbuds in and pretended I couldn't hear him.

Instead, I tried to stare him down and said, "Yes. I'm mad about the basketball."

"It was an accident," Caleb said. One of his eyebrows rose. "I wasn't aiming for you."

"Oh, well then," I said, rolling my eyes.

"It wasn't that big a deal." Caleb sounded annoyed, which was so frustrating I could have screamed. He was annoyed with me?

"Really?" I said.

"Really," he said. "Look, I'm sorry my friends laughed. But you had a funny expression. I was aiming for Donovan, not you, but instead of catching it, he ducked and ... " Caleb lifted one shoulder. "You didn't."

"You're sorry your friends laughed?" I stared at

him. "What kind of non-apology is that? Do you even know the definition of consequence?"

Caleb Khoury leaned away from me. It took him a couple of seconds more to react. Actually, it took him a lot of seconds. Finally, he crossed his arms and smiled at me. He actually *smiled*, like it was funny I was mad back at him.

"Okay," he said. "I'm sorry the basketball I threw at Donovan hit you instead and made you drop your books. I'm sorry the guys laughed at you. I said sorry at the time. Maybe you didn't hear me?" He uncrossed his arms and shrugged.

The shrug did it. I leaned forward, grabbed my backpack from under the chair in front of me, and yanked the zipper open. My phone was where it had been for the last ten days, in the inside pocket, and I pulled it out and showed it to him.

This time it didn't take him as along. When he saw the spiderweb of cracks across the whole screen, his smile vanished. He looked right at me, and it was a little startling to have Caleb Khoury's full attention.

Caleb's eyes were a really nice dark brown and they were sort of flicking back-and-forth.

"Did I do that?" he said.

He didn't *know*? Was that possible? My phone hit the ground after he'd tossed the basketball across the hallway and knocked everything out of my hands. When I'd picked it up, Donovan pointed at it and laughed. They'd all laughed and left, leaving me to pick up my books and binder. Donovan had even shoved Caleb and said, "Nice shot, Khoury!" and laughed his hyena laugh.

Had Caleb laughed? Had he seen? I couldn't remember.

"What do you think?" I said.

"Oh, wow," Caleb said. Finally, the guy seemed upset. "I didn't know. I swear."

I grunted, put the phone back and shoved it under the seat in front of me. I believed him, but that didn't make it any less frustrating, and it didn't do anything for how mad I was about it.

Raj would probably tell me I was holding on to a

bad mood on purpose because it was easier than letting it go.

Caleb didn't say anything else. He looked tense and upset, though. I guess he really hadn't seen my phone. I tried to listen to my inner Raj voice. It wasn't as good as the real Raj, but it was all I had right now. I took a deep breath. I considered pulling out my sketch pad but there was no way I was going to draw in front of Caleb Khoury.

Ugh. This train ride was going to suck beyond all telling.

"Why were you in Toronto?" Caleb said.

I turned, looking at him and trying to figure out if he really wanted to know, or if he was trying to smooth over the whole phone thing. I couldn't tell.

"My dad lives there," I said.

"Your dad moved to Toronto?" Caleb frowned. "Didn't Roy's parents hire him to redo their basement?"

"That's my stepdad, Mick," I said. I was surprised Caleb knew anything about me at all. We didn't exactly move in the same social circles, though we'd been in some of the same classes through most of high school. Then again, I knew his parents owned a couple of restaurants in Ottawa. I guess it wasn't strange he knew Mick worked in construction. It was written on the side of Mick's truck, and Mick sometimes picked me up from school if whatever job he was working on was nearby. And Caleb was right, Mick had worked for some of the other parents of kids at school.

"Oh," Caleb said. "So, you visit your dad on March Break?"

"Yeah," I said. "He gets me in Toronto for March Break, one week in summer, and one week over Christmas."

Caleb frowned again and did another one of those puppy head-tilt moves. "You don't like Toronto?"

"I don't really know anyone," I said, which was true. It was also easier than being completely honest about not really enjoying spending time with my father.

Caleb nodded. I hoped he was going to let this particular conversation drop. Surely his phone wasn't broken. Maybe he'd put in his own earbuds and leave me in peace.

"So, what does your dad do?"

I took a breath. Did he really want to talk to me about my father?

"He's an accountant," I said, and maybe I said it in the sharp way my mother calls "sass" because Caleb was clearly not going to let the conversation drop without a few clear hints I didn't want to talk about Toronto. Or my dad. Or anything, really, because whether or not he'd known about breaking my phone, he'd made an already bad week so much worse.

"And he didn't get your phone fixed?" Caleb said, that line back again between his eyebrows.

"He's not that kind of accountant," I said, annoyed at myself for defending my dad when I'd literally been stewing about the same fact back on the train station bench. "He works with small businesses, and taxes, and stuff. He's not a big corporate guy or rolling in it or anything." I sighed. "And he lives in Toronto, so his rent is really high."

Why was I saying all the things my father always said to me whenever money came up? I didn't really believe them when he said them to me, so why was I saying the same things to Caleb?

"Oh," Caleb said, and he kind of *winced*. It made me feel bad. Now I wanted to make *him* feel better. Ugh. Why was I like this?

"Okay, I don't know how true any of that is," I said. "I mean, he does work mostly with small businesses, and he never had any money to help me or my mom with anything, but I think it's more like he doesn't really care that much." When Caleb's dark-brown eyes widened, I had to look away. "It doesn't matter."

"That sucks," Caleb said.

"It's only three weeks a year," I said.

Caleb nodded slowly. "I guess."

The train started moving with a little lurch. I turned to stare out the window, watching as we moved out from under the covered area of the station. The sky was grey. Once we were clear of the station, the train started picking up speed. A few spatters of rain started to hit the window.

I wasn't even going to get nice views on the way home. I turned away from the window and caught

Caleb looking at me, but he looked out the window once I turned. He'd had a strange expression on his face, his lips were sort of tight in a straight line, and his eyes had almost been squinting at me.

Maybe he felt guilty about the phone?

"Something on my face?" Caleb said. He smiled a bit when he said it, though.

"No," I said, and turned away. I shoved my hands into the pockets of my hoodie.

This was going to be a long ride.

03 Caleb Khoury Never Shuts Up

"YOU'RE REALLY MAD AT ME," Caleb said.

It had been maybe five minutes since we'd left the station, and they'd been completely quiet until now. I'd been staring straight ahead. Not that I was looking at anything.

"I'm not," I said. Maybe saying it would make it true.

"You are," he said.

"Seriously?" I said, facing him. "Are you five?"

"Seriously?" Caleb said, grinning. He copied my voice. "Are you mad?"

Oh my God. He *was* a five-year-old.

"I believe you," I said. And I did believe him. It just didn't help much. "You didn't throw the basketball at me on purpose, and you didn't know you broke my phone." There. Maybe now he'd shut up.

"But you're still mad," Caleb said.

"I'm trying not to be," I said, pushing my head back in the chair. "But you're changing my mind."

"Wow," Caleb said. He poked my shoulder with one finger. "You're grumpier than I remember."

I rolled my head back to him. "Remember from when? You throwing a basketball at my head is the most we've interacted in . . . ever."

"I didn't throw it at your head. I threw it at Donovan's head. I missed." Caleb really seemed to think I didn't understand this. It was beyond annoying.

"Did you miss the whole speech Ms. Ryan gave us about impact versus intent?" I said. "I mean, you did a literal impact, Caleb."

His lips twitched, and then he smirked, and then he laughed out loud. I stared at him until he stopped, but it took a while.

"Are you always this brutally blunt?" Caleb said.

"Blunt?" It was my turn to laugh. No one would call me blunt. Ever. And definitely not brutal. "No. I never make waves." That was what Raj always said. *You never make waves, Ben.* I could hear them saying it in my head.

I was pretty sure it wasn't a compliment.

Caleb did his head-tilt again. "So, it's just me?"

"What?"

"Being blunt," Caleb said, pointing at me and then at himself. "This is an 'us' thing."

Us thing? I blew out a breath. "Why do you even care if I'm mad? In four hours and twenty minutes or so you'll never talk to me again, give or take a couple of weeks of school."

Caleb crossed his arms. "You don't like me, do you?"

"What was your first clue?" I snarked. The words popped out. I closed my mouth, surprised at myself. I never talked to people like this. What was wrong with me? Also, when Caleb crossed his arms, you could see how big his biceps were, even in the sleeves of the hoodie. It was distracting.

He took a deep breath. "Okay, I guess." He frowned at me. "It really was an accident."

"I know. You were aiming for Donovan," I said. "Your friend. Who is an asshole."

Caleb bit his lip. He was literally holding his bottom lip with his teeth. I could tell he wanted to give up and let me have the last word, but it was like he couldn't do it. "Okay, he's not always the best," he said, the words coming out in a rush. "But he's not a total asshole."

"He misgenders Raj on purpose," I said. "He's an asshole."

Caleb blinked. "He does?" He scowled, which surprised me. Caleb seemed to get how bad it was for someone to do that to Raj.

I felt a little bad. Again. How did Caleb Khoury keep making me feel bad for him? Was it his eyes? He did have puppy-dog eyes. "He does it indirectly, and with this totally fake friendly voice. Like, he'll see us standing at our lockers and say 'Hey, dudes,' or 'Hi, guys.'"

Caleb opened his mouth, and I knew what he was going to say, so I held up my hand. He stopped. Which was a surprise.

It was also kind of nice, actually. It was like Caleb realized one of us had more knowledge here, and it was me, so he should listen.

"Before you say 'dude' or 'guy' is a gender-neutral term, ask yourself how Donovan would react if we asked him which dude he was taking to Prom, or which guy his dad married, or how many dudes Donovan kissed on the weekend, or — "

"Right," Caleb said. "You're right. That's shitty." He frowned. "I'll talk to him."

Wait. What? I blinked. "You will?"

"I will," Caleb said. "For the record, he's never done it in front of me. So, obviously, he knows it's not cool."

"Oh," I said. I wasn't sure what else to say.

"So, is that why you don't like me?" Caleb asked. "Because Donovan is my friend?"

We were back to this? "I mean," I said, "it wasn't helping. The company you keep isn't always the nicest."

"That's rich," Caleb said. He snorted. "Half the people you hang out with are being total assholes to Jasmine."

Wait. Caleb knew Jasmine? I frowned at him, then remembered Jasmine's new boyfriend, Roy, was on the basketball team. Of course, he knew Jasmine, though he probably only really met her in February.

"You're right," I said. "They've been awful."

He glanced at me. One of his eyebrows rose. It felt a little like a taunt.

"Raj and I are trying to get them to see reason. Lin isn't even mad." I paused, considering my words. "Well, she's not mad about Jasmine and Roy because he's a guy. She's frustrated and sad because her girlfriend broke up with her." I shrugged. "And some of the others decided to turn it into a whole 'the Rainbow Club will stand by Lin' thing, which isn't right. When

Grayson and Ethan broke up, and Ethan found a new boyfriend at Canterbury, no one took sides."

"Because he was dating a *dude*," Caleb said, emphasizing the word I'd pointed out was definitely not gender-neutral.

"Right," I said. "Which is why this whole thing with Jasmine is wrong. It's biphobia."

Caleb looked at me, and his dark eyes were doing the flick-back-and-forth thing again. "Well, you talk to your people, and I'll talk to my people." He held out his hand. "Deal?"

Okay, what was happening? I took his hand and shook. No surprise, Caleb Khoury had a strong grip. "Deal," I said.

He let go. "So, you're done hating me?"

"Oh my God," I said, laughing. "I don't *hate* you. You just ruined my whole week, okay?"

He made a little grunting noise, then sat back in his seat again.

I took a breath, facing forward, and trying to figure out the whole conversation that had just happened.

Why had I told him all that stuff about Lin and Jasmine and Raj and Donovan?

Because he looked like he'd listen.

It wasn't rocket science. I'd had nine days with my father. I was *starving* for someone to listen to me, and Caleb Khoury seemed like he would listen.

And then he had.

"Okay, I have a question," Caleb said.

I laughed. "You actually can't sit quietly at all, can you?"

"True." Caleb shrugged. "Why didn't you fix your phone before you went to Toronto?"

"My dad got nonrefundable tickets," I said. "He didn't want to pay the fee for changing the day."

"Oh," Caleb said, nodding slowly. "Okay."

"Was that really bothering you?" I asked.

"Yeah," Caleb said. He had a crooked smile. One half of his mouth curved up more than the other, and it made him look like he was planning something silly. Or maybe something fun. Or both, probably. "I don't like mysteries."

"It's actually a perfect example of my father," I said. "No extra costs, ever. Not if it's something he thinks doesn't matter." When Caleb frowned, I went on, wanting to be clear. "He's not a deadbeat. He always pays child support. My mom never had to chase after him or anything. But he never offers a penny extra. Me and my mom learned not to ask for anything pretty quick." I shrugged. "I get the impression he's as excited for me to turn eighteen as I am."

"Because he doesn't have to pay after," Caleb said flatly. The smile was gone, and now it looked like he'd tasted something sour.

"Yep," I said. "But at least then I won't have to visit. This is officially my last March Break in Toronto."

"I'm sorry," Caleb said. "That sounds shitty."

"I don't think about it most of the time," I said, which was true. Other than the three weeks a year I was in Toronto, I didn't think about my dad much at all. Well, those three weeks and however long I dreaded going beforehand. That totalled maybe six weeks a year. Other than that, I didn't really think about it.

Caleb gave me another slow nod. "Do you have to go?"

"What?"

"To Toronto. Do you have to go?" Caleb looked at me. "Have you told your mom and stepfather you don't like it?"

"I . . . " I took a breath. "It's complicated."

"You should tell them," Caleb said, like it was the simplest thing in the world.

"Right," I said, not wanting to get into all the ways it wasn't simple at all. Like, what if I told my mother and Mick I didn't want to go but there wasn't a choice? That would upset my mom, and my mom being upset would upset Mick, and it would be for nothing.

This way, the only person who was upset was me, and I could handle it.

Ugh. New topic.

"This is the part where you tell me something bad about your parents," I said. "To even things out."

He cringed. "I can't."

"Okay," I said. "This is maybe why I hate you."

He stared, his eyes widening, and I couldn't maintain my poker face. I laughed.

"I'm kidding," I said.

"Wow, Benny," he said, shaking his head. "I had no idea you were this sarcastic. You're impressing me with all this venom."

"Shut up." I shook my head and rolled my eyes. *Benny*? No one called me Benny. Did I mind him calling me Benny?

"I can't shut up. We covered that," Caleb said, but then he did stay silent for a bit. We settled back. I kept waiting for him to pull out his own phone, but he didn't.

Should I tell him it was okay? Did he think it would bother me? Was I overthinking it?

Probably. You overthink everything. Raj's voice again. Raj's voice was getting a workout today.

"They're busy," Caleb said.

I didn't know what he meant. "Pardon?"

"My parents," Caleb said. "They're great, and I love them. I mean, y'know, they're still my parents and they get on my back about *everything*, but I know they're cool. But they run two restaurants, and it's a lot of work. So, I don't see them much." He faced me. "That's the worst I've got."

"I'd call Child Protective Services," I said, "if I had a phone."

He burst out laughing and put a hand over his chest. "You are not going to let that go, are you?"

"Never," I said, mostly because it would be funny to say.

"Well, I guess it gives me a lot of time to make it up to you," Caleb said.

Huh.

04 Caleb Khoury Takes Shots

THE FIRST TWO STOPS of the train ride back to Ottawa happen pretty quickly once you leave Toronto. They're both GO stations, and at the second one, someone got on board our car for the final empty seat.

Someone *cute*.

The new passenger had a retro black leather jacket that maybe didn't look warm enough for the slushy, rainy March weather, but was definitely cooler than anything I'd ever owned. The jacket had two thick white stripes on one arm and lots of zippers and pockets. The cute passenger didn't have a hat, which was probably because he'd styled his hair to do this tall, curly thing that was impressive and probably took a lot of styling gunk. He had great eyebrows that made me want to draw his face in an anime style. His eyes were dark, probably brown or hazel, and he had a great chin, the kind with a dent in it. And even from where I was sitting a few rows farther back, you could tell the guy had amazing eyelashes, too.

All together it made for a seriously cute guy. He slung his messenger bag off his shoulder and had it up in the compartment in no time. Then he sat, which ended my view.

"Here," Caleb said, and his voice made me jump. He was holding out a napkin.

I stared at it. "What's that for?"

He tapped his chin with his free hand. "You've got some drool. Right there."

I scowled at him. "I do not." Not exactly the best comeback.

"Uh-huh." Caleb laughed, then looked forward down the aisle. "You should say hi."

"What?" I said. He had to be kidding, right?

"I mean, you should take your shot," Caleb said it like it was the most normal thing in the world.

I stared at him. "People don't 'take their shot' on a train," I said. "That would be totally weird." I crossed my arms. "Besides, I don't even know if that guy would be into another guy. Or get pissed off at me for assuming he would." I wondered if it had ever occurred to Caleb what it was like when you were queer, like me. I doubted it. Caleb had been dating Emma Tremblay for almost a year now.

I wondered where he'd "taken his shot" with her.

"He had a pride pin on his jacket," Caleb said. "I think you're safe."

"He did?" I blinked. "I didn't see it."

"A maple leaf," Caleb said. "But a pride rainbow instead of red."

Okay, how in the world had Caleb noticed? For sure, I was a little distracted by the cute guy's face, but a rainbow maple leaf wasn't as obvious as a full pride flag. I stared at him, and Caleb stared right back, smirking. Caleb Khoury did smug really well. Like, it suited him.

So annoying.

"What?" he said.

"I'm trying to figure out how you noticed a subtle pride pin," I said. Because I couldn't figure out how Caleb Khoury was noticing pride symbols I missed. Make it make sense, please.

"My uncle and his husband have the same pin," Caleb said, lifting one shoulder.

"Oh," I said. "You have a gay uncle?"

"Two of them. Or, one, I guess. Uncle Gavin is bi." Caleb nodded. "They live in Toronto. I was visiting them." He shrugged again, but then he smiled. "They're great."

"That's cool," I said, trying to imagine what it would have been like to have someone in my own family I could have talked to about the whole gay thing. I bet it would have been *amazing*. My mother had been great about it when I came out. Mick, too. But it wasn't the same as having someone who understood. I hadn't had anyone until I got up the courage to join the Rainbow Club two years ago and met Raj and Jasmine and Lin and all the others.

"You don't sound like you mean it," Caleb said. He frowned like maybe I'd offended him.

"Oh no," I said, shaking my head. "No, I just . . ." I wasn't sure what to say, exactly.

"You just what?" Caleb said.

"Honestly?" I said, deciding the whole blunt thing I'd been doing was the way to go. Like I'd said earlier, I only had to sit with Caleb for the next four hours or so. So, what if I said what I actually thought for a change? "I'm jealous."

"Oh," he said. Now I'd surprised him. "Jealous of . . . ?" He shook his head like he didn't get it.

"Having queer uncles. I think it would have been nice," I said. "Don't get me wrong. My mom handled it really well. Mick, too, and he's this big burly construction worker dude, and even though I thought he'd be okay, I was worried. But having someone already out in the family would have been . . . " I shook my head. I didn't have words. I didn't even know where to begin imagining having someone there who'd already faced all the stuff heading my way. Someone I could talk to who'd actually already been there? Yeah. There were no words. "It would have been cool."

"Your dad didn't handle it well?" Caleb said. I guess he'd noticed I hadn't mentioned him.

"He didn't take it as well as my mom," I said. "But he wasn't bad about it or anything. He was surprised. Which always amazes me, because . . . " I waved a hand at myself.

"What?" Caleb said, frowning.

"People have been calling me gay since I was *four*, Caleb," I said. "They knew before I did."

He shook his head. "Really?"

"Well, I don't think they were trying to be helpful in my coming out journey, no." I pulled off my glasses and wiped them on my hoodie. "They were being mean. But people have always seemed to just *know*. Guys especially. I don't know why." I shrugged. "Maybe it's my face."

Caleb stared at my face. "What about it?" He looked like he was trying to figure out what part of my face said 'Gay!'

"I don't really know," I said. "I mean, my smile maybe? Or my ears?" I've always thought I smiled funny. My teeth show too much. And my ears stick out a bit.

Caleb shook his head. "I don't think that's it." Then he grinned. "Maybe it's the drool on your chin whenever you see a cute guy."

"Shut up!" I said, but couldn't help myself from glancing at the back of Cute Guy's head.

"You were wrong about people not taking their shots on a train, by the way," Caleb said. "I'm pretty sure my uncle Scott met Uncle Gavin on a train."

"You're making that up," I said.

"Well. Kind of. They met on the TTC. But it's still a train." Caleb crossed his arms like he'd won some sort of victory. He was so annoying. And every time he crossed his arms, I couldn't help staring at his biceps, and I was sure he was going to notice.

Then again, given he had queer uncles and seemed to like them, if he did spot me checking out his arms, he probably wouldn't be actually *mad* or anything. That was something.

He'd probably give me a napkin again and be all smug.

"I highly doubt your uncle randomly approached someone on the TTC," I said.

"It was right after Pride," Caleb said. "Gavin had a rainbow painted on his face."

"Oh," I said. "Well. Okay. Yeah. Fine. That's different, obviously."

"How?" Caleb said. He pointed toward the front of the train car. "He has a rainbow on his jacket. So, you can go take your shot."

"Please stop saying that," I said. "It's not going to happen."

"Why not?" Caleb said.

"Because I like to keep my monthly humiliation down to a minimum," I said. "You already maxed it out with a basketball."

"Oh my God," Caleb threw his head back, laughing. "Let it go, Benny." He turned back to me, leaning in. "Go say hi."

"If you're so obsessed with the cute boy," I said, crossing my arms. "You go talk to him."

Caleb narrowed his eyes. "Is that a dare?"

"What?"

"Is that a dare?" Caleb said.

What was even happening right now? "Sure," I said. "Totally a dare. Caleb Khoury, go talk to the cute boy."

Caleb uncrossed his arms and shook out his wrists, twisting his head left and then right and making his neck pop. Ew. Then he unzipped his hoodie.

"What are you doing?" I asked.

Caleb just smiled at me, pulling off his hoodie. Underneath, he had a plain white T-shirt on. It was really unfair how good he looked in a plain white T-shirt. It showed off how wide his shoulders already were, and his arms were even more impressive than before once you could see the curve of his biceps pull the edges of his sleeves tight.

When I wore a white T-shirt, I just looked like I'd forgotten to pack a sweater.

He stood up, putting the hoodie on the seat. He ran a hand through his hair.

"Caleb," I said, frowning. "Seriously. What are you doing?"

"I am taking my shot, Benny," he said. Then Caleb Khoury winked at me and started off down the aisle of the train car toward the cute guy.

05 Caleb Khoury Is Into Guys

"CALEB!" I whispered, but he kept going.

Oh my God. Was he actually going to go talk to Cute Guy? *Why?* If he was trying to prove something to me, it made no sense. For one, Caleb Khoury had been dating Emma for almost a year now, so it wasn't like he was going to go get the guy's number. Also, Cute Guy was a *guy*. If he thought showing me it was no big deal to talk to Cute Guy would score him some kind of win, he'd missed the point.

Of course, guys could talk to each other. Especially when one of the guys was Caleb Khoury. He was handsome, and in good shape, and was, y'know, *a guy*.

But if I did it, there was the danger the other guy might realize I was gay, and if he didn't like that . . .

Well.

I was leaning over in my seat to see down the aisle. Caleb was almost at Cute Guy's spot. He was two seats away. One seat. He was right beside him . . .

Caleb kept walking.

I sat up straight and blew out a big breath. What a jerk. Lifting a bit, I saw Caleb get to the far end of the train car and go into the small bathroom there. Of course.

"Taking my shot," I muttered. "Right. More like taking a shit."

I stared at the closed bathroom door. When Caleb was finished and started back, I was going to level the best glare I could manage. When he sat down, I was going to tell Caleb Khoury to his face he was a total asshole.

Which was so unlike me I almost reconsidered it. Then his smug, smiling face appeared again, and he started sauntering back down the aisle. I rose enough in my seat to start glaring. He didn't seem to care I was glaring at him. In fact, he wasn't looking at me. He was looking at Cute Guy.

Wait.

No way.

When Caleb got to the cute guy's seat, he stopped walking and said something. Caleb smiled, and sort of leaned on the back of the seat in front of where the cute guy was sitting.

Oh. My. God. He *was* talking to the guy. And *posing*. When he laughed at something the cute guy said, Caleb rubbed the back of his neck with one hand, which I'd seen him do before when he was with Emma. It was a good look on him. Bashful and cute. And, of course, lifting his hand made it impossible to miss how nice his arms were.

The white T-shirt was definitely working for Caleb Khoury.

I slid back down in my chair. I couldn't hear what they were saying, though I did hear Caleb laugh once, then twice. I wanted to pull my hood over my head and tug the strings until I couldn't see. I was dying of second-hand embarrassment.

Or was it jealousy?

Either way, I was going to die on this train. Any second now.

A few minutes later, Caleb dropped into the seat beside me. He rolled his head to the side to look at me, a giant grin on his face.

"What is wrong with you?" I hissed.

He lifted his shoulders. "I complimented him on his pin."

"Oh," I said. That wasn't a bad opener. Despite myself, I wanted to know what they'd talked about. "What's Cute Guy's name?"

"I don't know," Caleb said. He frowned. "I can't believe I forgot to ask."

"Really?" I stared at him.

"I got nervous," he said, and he actually *blushed*.

Nervous? Why would he get nervous? It wasn't like he was being serious.

"Does Emma know you randomly talk to cute guys on trains?" I said, crossing my arms and trying to mirror his pose. It didn't work. I'm pretty sure I looked goofy, not impressive.

"We broke up." Caleb looked down.

"Oh," I said. "Sorry." I maybe didn't sound very sincere. Like, at all. I really didn't like Emma Tremblay.

"Wow." Caleb stared at me, eyes wide. "And you said I didn't know how to apologize."

I cringed. That was totally fair. "Let me try again," I said. "I'm sorry you had a breakup. I didn't mean to remind you."

Caleb stared at me for a few seconds. "You don't like her, do you?"

"You seem to care an awful lot about who I like and don't like," I said.

"That's not an answer. You do that a lot. You say something, but you don't answer the question." He crossed his arms, which made me look at his biceps again. I forced myself to look back up at his face.

Stupid white T-shirt.

"Okay," I said. "But first tell me if you're really upset, or if you want to get back together with her?"

"Why?" he said, frowning.

"Because I don't want to put my foot in my mouth."

Caleb shifted in his seat to face me. He pressed his shoulder into the back of the chair and pulled one leg up onto the seat. "I don't think we're going to get back together," he said. "No, I don't want to. I don't think so, anyway." He sighed. "No."

I wondered if that was the first time he'd said it out loud.

"She's kind of cruel," I said.

He blinked. "Emma?"

I nodded. "She's smart," I said. "But she's mean about being smart."

He shook his head. "I don't get it."

"Do you have any classes with her?" I asked.

"Just history," he said.

"Okay," I said. "Well, in Algebra, if someone doesn't understand something, she gets annoyed. And she's really obvious about it."

"Obvious?" Caleb said. He was frowning again. And he seemed uncomfortable.

I wondered if he already knew what I was talking about.

"I'm not smart," I said.

He shook his head. "Sure you are."

"Thanks, but I'm not," I said, holding up a hand before he could argue. "It's okay that I'm not smart. When it comes to Math? History? Biology? Anything that's memorizing stuff, I have to study. I have to practise so much, and then if I'm lucky I get a B. I barely understood what I was doing in Math in grade nine, and it hasn't gotten better." I took a breath because I didn't usually tell people this. I mean, I told Raj, but Raj and I were best friends. And they understood I wasn't asking them to make me feel better, I just needed to say these things out loud to someone who wasn't going to tell me I could do better if I tried harder or worked smarter.

My dad loved that one. "Don't work harder, work smarter, Ben." What did that even mean? Of course, I'd like to work smarter! My brain, however, didn't know how.

Caleb, though, didn't tell me to try something different. He didn't argue with me, either. He nodded. "Okay."

Huh. Just like Raj. I'd really expected Caleb to be the kind of guy who needed to fix a problem. I'd expected Caleb would see my almost-B average as a problem, rather than a hard-won victory.

"Um," I said, trying to remember what the point had been. Emma. Right. "Well, when I asked questions in class, trying to figure something out, Emma would make these little noises. She'd sigh. Or she'd groan. Roll her eyes." I waved a hand. "She let everyone know she already understood, and it was *so annoying* I didn't." I shrugged. "It's mean. I need to ask questions if I'm going to pass. I don't care if someone like Emma Tremblay finds me annoying. But I bet there are other people who don't ask questions because of her."

Caleb didn't say anything for a while. The rain hit the window behind me, and the sound was really loud all of a sudden.

Caleb swallowed. "I'm sorry."

"It wasn't you," I said. "But thank you." I felt bad for throwing a downer on Caleb and tried to think of another topic of discussion. I glanced forward and saw the back of Cute Guy's head again. "What are you going to do if Cute Guy turns out to be interested?" I said.

"What?" Caleb looked startled.

"You were doing some first-class flirting up there," I said. I put my arm behind my head and rubbed my neck, which didn't make me feel all cool or bashful in the slightest. I hammed it up a bit.

"Dude, stop," Caleb said, cringing. "Did I really look like that?"

"No." I snorted. "Of course, you didn't." Caleb looked great. Like he always did. "I'm sure he thought you were great."

"You think?" Caleb said, and his voice had a little hitch.

"Wait." I stared at him. What was happening? "Do you *want* him to think you were great?"

"Maybe?" Caleb said. "I mean, I'm not opposed to it." He was blushing. Caleb Khoury was blushing. He shrugged. "It would be okay, yeah."

The word thunderstruck did not cover what was happening in my brain right now. "Wait. Are you saying you're . . . ?" I said.

He lifted one shoulder. "Yeah."

Stop the damn train. Caleb Khoury was into guys?

"Oh," I said. I kind of squirmed, too. "Sorry. I didn't know. Really. I wasn't making fun, I promise."

He laughed. "It's okay, I don't really tell a lot of people. I mean, some of my friends know I'm bi, kinda."

"Kinda?" I said.

"Kinda," he said.

Okay. Well, that cleared nothing up.

"Thank you for telling me." That was something we practised at the Rainbow Club. Thanking people who trusted us enough to tell us about their queerness. "And don't worry. I won't tell anyone."

He nodded, but I couldn't tell if he'd been worried I would tell people or not.

We stared at each other. Then, because I didn't have the slightest clue what else to say, I said, "Was that the first time you ever flirted with a guy?"

"Maybe?" he said, and he squinted. "Yes. I guess. It was weird. It was different. Why was it different?" Caleb scowled like he was so used to being so cool around girls that *not* being cool around boys offended him somehow. "It shouldn't be different."

"Of course, it's different," I said. "All the rules are gone."

"Rules?"

"Open the door. Pull out the chair. The father gives away the bride." I shrugged. "There are so many rules for straight people, telling them what to do. It's different for us."

Us. I'd just used the word *us* to describe myself and Caleb Khoury. How was this my life? What was even happening right now?

"I didn't propose, Benny," he said, with a little snort. "I said he had a nice pin."

"I know," I said. "But think about how many different versions you've seen of 'guy flirts with girl.' Shows. Movies. Examples of what to say, what to do." I smiled. "And what *not* to say, what *not* to do."

He seemed to be honestly considering it. "I guess."

"It's also fun, though," I said. "It's one of the best things, really. No rules." I tilted my head. "I mean, once you get over the terror of it all."

That made Caleb laugh. "Right." He faced me. "You're being pretty cool about this."

I blinked. "Why wouldn't I be? Wait. Caleb, you do know I'm . . . " I did jazz hands. "Gay."

"If I hadn't, the drool would have given it away," Caleb said, but this time he didn't smile. "I guess, the whole Jasmine thing made me wonder how you might react."

The Jasmine thing? It took me a second to realize he meant Jasmine dating Roy, and the way the Rainbow Club had been acting. "No, no," I said. "Like I said, that's some biphobia bullshit. I hate the way people are treating her." I really did, too. "Wait. Is that why you don't tell anyone else?"

"Not really." He shook his head. "It's more like I was already with Emma so . . . why bother? Why ask for drama, you know?"

"Hm." I tried to sound understanding. I really did. But I'm the kid everyone knew was gay just by looking at me. My sympathy for Caleb Khoury's wanting to 'avoid drama' wasn't very high.

I doubt I sounded convincing. Caleb turned away, and he didn't say anything for a while. The rain got even louder against the window. It was really coming down out there. It fit the mood. Caleb's breakup. Jessica and Lin's breakup. Caleb being in the closet. Me never really having the option of being in the closet.

Not that being in the closet was good or anything. Ugh.

"It was kind of why we broke up," Caleb said. He was staring at the seat in front of him, but I didn't think he was actually seeing it.

"Sorry?" I didn't follow.

"I asked Emma if we could bring Scott with us to Prom. Make it a group thing," he said.

"You thought *Emma* wouldn't mind doing a group friend thing for Prom?" I said, and, okay, maybe I did a terrible job hiding my amazement at how much he should have known better.

He blew out a breath. "Why does everyone say it like that?"

"I mean, have you *met* her?" I said, lifting one hand. Emma Tremblay was not the sort to do anything that would take away from being the centre of attention at the best of times, but at her own prom night?

He crossed his arms and glared at me, which would have been intimidating if he hadn't laughed a moment later. Then he leaned in closer, and his voice dropped. "Fine. You're right. I felt bad about Scott not having anyone to go with. He's the only guy on the whole team who didn't have a date. We're tight. He's such a good guy. I don't get why he's single. Anyway, I didn't think it would be a big deal if he went with us. But she didn't understand. She thought I meant . . ." He blushed again. He lifted one shoulder and uncrossed his arms. He waved one hand in a way that said. 'you know,' but I didn't know.

It took me way longer than it should have to get it. When I finally did, I barked out a laugh.

"*A prom threesome?*" I exclaimed. It came out way too loud.

"Uh," a voice said.

We both looked up. Cute Guy was standing right beside Caleb in the aisle.

06 Caleb Khoury Eats a Lot

"OH," Caleb said. "Hey."

I couldn't say anything. If I was lucky, maybe the train would derail, and we could all die a fiery death.

"Hey," Cute Guy said. He was even cuter up close, but he pointed farther down the train and then kept walking. I had zero doubt he'd come to say something to Caleb, but he'd clearly just changed his mind.

Because I'd basically yelled "*prom threesome!*" at him.

Caleb turned his head to stare at me, his mouth open.

"Sorry," I said. Then I lost it and started laughing. It was so awful, but it was also kind of incredible, and then Caleb was laughing, too.

Caleb Khoury had a great laugh. His whole body seemed to be in on it, he had to lean forward, putting his hands over his face while he shook with it. For my part, I had my hand over my mouth, trying to at least be quiet for the other passengers. It took us a bit to calm down, but then Cute Guy passed by again in the other direction. He didn't even look at us.

That set us off again, and this time I had tears running down my cheeks.

Poor guy. He'd probably gone into the bathroom at the other end of the train long enough to wash his hands or something, to make it look like that was what he'd been going to do all along.

"Well," Caleb said, wiping his face. "I'm pretty sure you ruined my shot." He chuckled. "I don't think he wants to join our prom threesome."

I snorted again and shook my head. "I'm so sorry. Really." My eyes were still running. I barely stopped myself from laughing again.

"Oh, I can tell," Caleb said. "Benny, you're the worst wingman ever." He shook his head and glanced down the train.

I should have felt worse about ruining his chances with Cute Guy, but I didn't. Also, when I looked at him, I didn't think Caleb looked upset. If anything, Caleb actually seemed relieved, maybe.

"So," I said. "Are you and Scott going to hit Prom together, then? As friends?"

Caleb tilted his head. "That's not a bad idea. We could ask some other people, too, maybe." He turned to me. "I'm guessing you and Raj are going together?"

"No," I said, a little confused. Me and Raj? "The Rainbow Club is doing a group thing," I said. "Or we were, before the whole Jasmine and Lin breakup happened. Going as a group means none of us had to go alone. Myself included."

"Wait. Did you and Raj break up?" He rolled his

head to the side to look at me.

"Raj and I were never together," I said, surprised. "They're my best friend."

"Really?" Caleb blinked.

"Really," I said.

"Benny, the *whole school* thinks you two are dating," Caleb said.

"What?" I stared at him. My mouth opened, but no words came out. "Me and Raj? People think we're *dating*?" I said. I hadn't realized people thought about me at all.

"You hang out with Raj all the time. You sit together. I've seen you drawing with them. When you hang out outside in the field, Raj leans on your shoulder. And you two hug and sort of cuddle. A lot." Caleb lifted both hands. "It paints a picture, Benny."

"Oh," I said. I didn't know what else to say. Also, how in the world had Caleb Khoury noticed all that stuff?

"That's probably why no one else asked you to Prom," Caleb said, pointing a finger gun at me. "You two look like you're dating."

"There are no people waiting to ask me out, I promise you." I laughed. "I'm not that interesting."

Caleb leaned back. "What do you mean, not that interesting?"

"I'm not." I took a breath because for some reason I really wanted Caleb to understand. This wasn't a pity party or anything. "I don't mind. I'm not upset with who I am or anything." Well, most of the time I wasn't. But who was happy with who they were all the time? "But . . . " I looked around, trying to figure out how to put it, and then realized I was literally sitting in an example. "I'm like this train," I said.

"You're a train?" Caleb said. He squinted.

"I go where I'm supposed to go," I said. "Back-and-forth, same tracks, on schedule. No surprises." I shrugged. "I'm reliable. You can count on me. And that's okay. Trains are okay." I felt a little proud of my metaphor. Or was it a simile? I could never remember which was which.

Caleb took a second before he said anything. I'd

STUCK WITH YOU

noticed it was a habit of his, and it was a nice one. He listened, thought about things, and then replied.

"Bullet trains," he said.

"Sorry?"

"Some trains are exciting," Caleb said. "Bullet trains. They go, like, hundreds of kilometres an hour."

"No one would confuse me with a bullet train," I said.

"You are too blunt and too sarcastic to be a regular train," Caleb said, shaking his head. "I have learned that about you. Benny the Bullet Train, all the way."

I laughed. Honestly? It was a nice thought. "If only there was a bullet train to the Prom," I said, shifting the topic. "Then I wouldn't be arguing with everyone."

"You're arguing?"

"Arguing is maybe too strong a word," I admitted. I'd started to ask Grayson if we weren't being unfair to Jasmine, and he cut me off, and then I shut up and walked away. So, it was definitely not arguing. I still felt like crap for not saying more, and it had bothered me all week. "I want Jasmine and Roy to come with us. Jasmine is a member of the Rainbow Club, and she helped organize getting our limo and everything. I brought it up, but I kind of got shot down and then . . . " I sighed. "Like you said. I need to talk to them."

You never make waves, Ben.

"Well," Caleb said. "It's not too late, right?"

I nodded. "No. It's not. And we did shake on it." I smiled, even though I didn't feel confident in the slightest. Caleb could probably tell because he got a little quiet again.

I eyed the rain, which wasn't letting up, and shifted in my seat. I really did need to speak up. I needed to face down the club and tell them flat out we needed to make it clear Jasmine and her boyfriend were welcome to come with us because she was a part of our club. I'd probably stutter, and maybe throw up, but I needed to do it.

I hated arguing with people. Especially my friends.

A tall, grey-haired man with a little gold nametag started making his way down the aisle with the trolley of drinks and snacks, and Caleb pulled up his foldout table from his armrest. When he got to us, Caleb bought a coffee, and I checked my pockets for change and got a tea. I had a half-dozen oatmeal raisin cookies in my bag and pulled them out.

After the man had moved on, Caleb gave me a sideways glance. "You drink tea?" he said.

"I drink tea." I didn't have to explain myself, but I ended up doing it, anyway. "I can't drink coffee," I said. "Instant headache."

He blinked. "Really?"

"Really," I said. "Chocolate, too."

Caleb cringed, putting a hand on his chest. His dark eyes widened dramatically. The guy could really ham it up. "You can't eat *chocolate*?"

"I can eat white chocolate," I said.

He grimaced. "But why would you?"

"Because regular chocolate gives me headaches so bad, I barf," I said.

"I'd still consider it," he said, tipping his head one way, then the other.

"No, you wouldn't," I said. I knew he was just

kidding. Maybe it was dumb to get annoyed. People who didn't have migraines had no idea what it was like, but that wasn't their fault.

He frowned. "That bad?"

"That bad," I said. I was being one hundred percent honest, too. I offered him a cookie, and he took it. "It's not fun. I get a warning, and I have medication. It works most of the time."

"You get a warning?" He'd already eaten half his cookie. Caleb Khoury could *eat*.

"Aura," I said, and waved my fingers in front of my eyes. "There's this white light that sort of spreads around in my eyes. It's hard to explain, but I can't see right. It blocks other stuff out. Once I start seeing it, I need to take my meds and get somewhere dark and quiet, drink some water, and breathe through it. If I'm quick enough, I can skip the migraine." I took a bite of my first cookie.

"English class in grade nine," Caleb said, looking at me. "You had to leave. You were shaking, and sweating. Was that a migraine?"

"The start of one, yeah." I was surprised he remembered. It had been one of those times I hadn't been quick enough, and I'd ended up going home sick. It had been really bad in grade nine for some reason. It felt like I'd had to go home once a month or so, and I'd had migraines once or twice a week, though most of them happened after school, thankfully.

Caleb polished off a second cookie before I finished my first, then turned back to face me.

"If they don't change their minds," he said. "Maybe Roy and Jasmine could come with me and Scott and whoever else I can round up at the last minute." He sighed. "I already paid for the car."

It took me a second to realize what he meant. He was talking about inviting Jasmine and Roy to go to Prom with him. If I didn't change the Rainbow Club's minds about Jasmine bringing Roy, he'd offer to have them go with him.

It was strange. It made me happy and sad at the same time. It made me happy he'd offer. But it made me sad my friends weren't living up to their own promises.

"I'll change their minds," I said.

He gave me an odd look. Then he glanced down at my little foldout table and back up at me.

"What?" I said.

"Can I have another cookie?"

07 Caleb Khoury Makes Text Noises

I GAVE CALEB a third cookie, and his phone pinged while he ate it. He pulled it out but then froze. He bit his lip.

"Is it okay if I . . . ?" he said.

It took me a second to realize he was asking me to let him use his phone.

I crossed my arms. "Really? Right in front of me? Way to rub salt in the wound, Khoury." I was obviously kidding.

He snorted and started answering the text while he ate the cookie. After the cookie, he dug around in his bag and pulled out an apple, and ate that, too. Then a granola bar, which he offered to split with me, but I waved off. The dude did not stop eating the entire time he was texting, and the frown on his face made it clear he wasn't having a good conversation.

Also, it turned out Caleb grunted when he sent texts. Every text he sent went off with a little grunting noise. Like he was adding a tiny bit of attitude with every text message.

Was he mad?

I wanted to ask, but I also knew it was none of my business. I heard Raj's voice again. *You never make waves, Ben.* I turned my gaze out the window and stared at almost nothing. Usually, by now, there were nice views of the lake. Instead, the rain was still coming down hard, and you could barely see past the windows. It felt like we'd slowed down, too. I wondered if we were going to be late arriving in Ottawa.

Caleb grunted and texted for a long while. After

my tea, I closed my eyes for a bit, but I wasn't sleepy enough, even with the rain hitting the window.

"Sorry," Caleb said.

I opened my eyes. "For what?"

He held up his phone, then slid it back into his pocket.

"You sounded mad," I said.

"I'm not mad," he said, shaking his head. He blew out a breath. "It was Emma."

"Ah," I said. I wondered if he'd tell me more, but I didn't want to ask.

He glanced at me. "She wants the car."

"The car?" I said, not following. Then it clicked. "Oh. For Prom." I frowned. "Wait, do you mean she wants it, wants it? Like, not to go with you, but to take it from you?"

He nodded. "Yep."

"Wow," I said. I mean, it was very on-brand for Emma, but it took some confidence to ask.

"She says I should know she cares more about this than I do," Caleb said. "That I'm being unreasonable."

"Didn't you pay for it?" I said. Prom cars weren't cheap.

He lifted one shoulder. "It's not that."

Must be nice not to have to care about the price tag. I waited. But he didn't say anything else. He leaned back in his seat, arms crossed, and I wondered if he was trying to come up with a way to explain for me or if we were done talking about it. Either way, I didn't have a lot to contribute here.

Caleb's stomach gurgled. It was really loud, and I tried not to laugh, but a little snicker came out.

He narrowed his eyes. "What?"

"I'm amazed you're hungry," I said. "Three cookies, an apple, a granola bar, a cup of coffee . . . " I tapped off on my fingers.

"It's lunch time," he said, but he smiled when his stomach gurgled again, and I laughed. He rummaged in his bag and pulled out a sub, unwrapping it and digging in. It looked like it had every possible topping on it, and it smelled surprisingly good for a duffel-bag sub.

I'd brought a small tub of pasta salad. I pulled it out

and found the plastic fork I'd tucked in my bag and set to it. My mind was still on the prom car thing, though. One of the reasons we'd decided to do a Rainbow Club group was how expensive it was to rent a car for Prom. I'd be mad if someone expected me to hand over something I'd paid for. It didn't surprise me Emma thought Caleb should give her the car, though.

I wondered what it was like to not have to worry so much about having enough money for things. My family wasn't poor, and we didn't struggle, but I was looking at college or university and the idea of taking out a loan made me feel sick, especially since I wasn't sure I'd manage to succeed at more school. My mom and stepdad didn't have extra cash, either. They'd bought the house when they'd gotten married and then they'd had my two sisters. Mom had done maternity leave both times, and when she went back to work again, they'd moved her from school to school for a while. Mick worked hard, and he did well for himself, but I was pretty sure most of the money from his job went to the mortgage.

I'd never asked if they could help me once I graduated high school, but I had told them I'd planned to take a gap year to get money in the bank instead of taking out a loan. My mom said she was proud of me. Mick told me he could get me a job with his crew, again, like last summer.

I hadn't given him a yes or no on that front yet.

"You have think-face," Caleb said, sub halfway to his mouth.

"Think-face?" I asked. "What's think-face?"

He chewed a bite of his sub, then scrunched up his face, twisting his lips to one side.

"You look like you need the bathroom," I said.

"Is that what you're thinking about?" he asked.

"No," I said. "Gap year."

"You're taking a gap year?" He took another bite. His sub was already half gone. Okay, Caleb Khoury was the fastest eater I'd ever met.

"Yeah," I said.

"That's cool," Caleb said, smiling. "I wish my parents would let me take a year off."

"That's not what I'm doing," I said, annoyed. *A year off?* Did he really think I was going to play video games and sleep in for a year?

Caleb bit his lip. "Sorry." He seemed to realize he'd said something wrong, but I didn't think he knew what it was. "Again. Because all I do is make you mad."

"That's not true," I said. It came out in my grumpy voice though.

"Uh-huh," Caleb smirked. "So. What are you doing?"

"I'll be working," I said. "With Mick, if I can't find something else. If I do decide I'm going to college, I need to pay for it."

Caleb finished his sub. He crumpled up the wrapper and looked at me. "You might not go?"

"College, maybe. I am definitely not going to university," I said, shaking my head.

"Well, that's something," Caleb said.

"It is?" I asked. I stabbed the last of my pasta on my fork and took a final bite. I hated not having any idea of what it was I was supposed to do next. Everyone else seemed to know where they were going and what they'd be doing. I only seemed to ever know what I *didn't* want to do.

"Sure," Caleb said. "My dad says it's important to know things you don't want as much as it is the stuff you do."

"Well, I know I don't want to go to university," I said. My mother had flinched like I'd broken her heart when I'd told her. I'd only made it better by saying I'd consider college. Mick went to college. He graduated from a trade school. And Mick had a great job.

Of course, I didn't have the slightest clue what "great job" I wanted.

"Well, sometimes you gotta make it up on the fly," Caleb said.

"I never make things up on the fly," I said. "I don't think my brain works that way."

He laughed like I'd told a joke, but I was pretty sure it was the truth.

"What are you doing after graduation?" I asked, mostly to stop thinking about how I didn't know what I was doing after school.

He pulled a water bottle from his bag and flipped the straw up. He swallowed before he started talking again. "There's no way my parents will let me take a gap year, but this summer I'm going to work at the restaurants again. They want me to get more involved. See if I want in on the family business."

"Do you?" I asked.

"I don't know," he said. "But if I don't like it, that's okay. I can figure out something else."

I wondered what it was like to have that sort of confidence. I bet he didn't stay up at night thinking of all the things he couldn't do. I bet Caleb Khoury went to bed and actually fell asleep right away. Also, he probably slept in his underwear. He didn't strike me as a pyjama bottoms kind of guy. Or did he even wear underwear to bed? When he looked at me again, he frowned. "What? You have think-face again."

"Nothing," I said, embarrassed. Was he a boxers guy? I bet he was a boxers guy.

"What *do* you like to do?" he said. "What's a job you'd like?"

I shook my head. "Better people than you have tried to turn my hobbies into a job, Caleb."

"Ouch," he said, pressing a hand to his chest. "Man, you think so little of me, don't you?"

I lifted one shoulder, putting the fork in my container and closing it instead of answering.

"Seriously," he said. "What are you good at?"

I sighed. "Not much." I smiled when I said it, though. "Seriously. Name a class, and I promise I had to study my butt off to pass it."

"Art," he said.

I blinked. Huh. "Okay," I said. "I love Art class." I didn't have to study for it, either. I wasn't going to admit it to Caleb, though.

"I know." He grinned, which was super annoying. "I see you drawing all the time, remember?"

"I'm not going to be a professional artist," I said. This was always my father's suggestion, too. Graphic design. Marketing. *Take something you're good at and enjoy and make it into a job, Ben!*

"Why not?" Caleb said. Instead of sounding like

he was arguing with me, he sounded like he wanted to know.

Not like my dad.

"I draw for fun," I said. "To relax. I like it. When I do it on a deadline, it's different." I knew I wasn't being very clear. I tried again. "When you're playing basketball with your friends, it's fun, right? But I bet it feels different when you're in an actual tournament."

Caleb nodded slowly. "I get it." He tilted his chin. "Okay, you're not going to do art. That's fine. What are you going to try instead?" He looked at me, waiting.

"I don't know," I said. "That's the problem. Everyone else seems to have a plan, but . . ." I shrugged. "I don't."

"That's not true," Caleb said. "You're taking a gap year. You're working. That's a plan."

"Tell it to my mother," I said, raising one eyebrow.

"Sure," he said. "I'll come by."

I laughed.

"Benny, I will," Caleb said, shoving my shoulder. "Parents *love* me."

"Oh, I bet," I said.

"I convinced Donovan's mom to let him go on the senior trip this year, even after his whole hangover-barfing-on-the-bus thing last year," Caleb said. "I am *magic* at parents." He drank more water.

The thing was, I believed him. I bet parents really did love Caleb Khoury. Caleb Khoury was the kind of son I bet most parents secretly hoped they would have. He was a decent student. He was a more than decent athlete. Other kids liked him. He laughed a lot. I could almost hate him a little.

But it wasn't just that.

You're taking a gap year. You're working. That's a plan.

It was strange, but when Caleb said it, it sounded true.

08 Caleb Khoury Never Sits Still

WE STOPPED IN COBOURG, and a few people got off the train. The server guy took our empty cups. I thought about trying to have a nap. When I turned my head to the window and closed my eyes, though, it didn't work. I was still thinking about gap years and college and university.

I so wasn't going to be able to sleep.

Instead, I looked out the window and watched the rain hitting the glass. It was absolutely pouring.

I sat up again.

"Not tired?" Caleb asked.

"Apparently not." I lifted one shoulder. It was too embarrassing to tell him the truth. Raj called it *stewing*. And Raj was right. I was stewing over things I couldn't figure out. But until I figured them out, I didn't know what else to do.

You're taking a gap year. You're working. That's a plan.

Caleb's phone chimed. He sighed, pulled it out, read it, and then put it back in his pocket.

"Not going to answer?" I asked.

"Apparently not." He lifted one shoulder. Then he smiled.

"I see what you did there," I said.

"This is torture," Caleb said, leaning back in his chair and puffing out a breath. "We're going so slow."

"Not a fan of the train?" I asked.

"Not a fan of sitting still," he said. He eyed me. "I don't know how you do it."

"Sit still?" I laughed. "Well, I sit down, and then I decide not to move." I lifted both hands like I was doing a magic trick. "Ta-da."

"You're funny," he said, rolling his eyes, but at least he was smiling again.

Wait. When did it start mattering if Caleb Khoury was smiling?

"Seriously, though. I'm not good at being bored," Caleb said. His left leg was bouncing in place.

"I can tell," I said.

"Huh?" he said.

I pointed at his bouncing leg. He stopped. He let out a little groan, then took a deep breath. "This is why I will never have a desk job," he said. "Can you picture me sitting in a cubicle?"

"I'm pretty sure whoever was in the cubicle beside you would probably murder you." I lifted one shoulder. "So, it wouldn't be for long."

"Oh man, I'm being annoying, aren't I?" He bit his bottom lip and squinted, and honestly, it was way too good a look on him. How was it some guys could be so cute when they were also being a lot? Not that I exactly blamed him. The train had been crawling along instead of the usual speed, and the rain made for a boring view out the window.

"You're not being annoying," I said. "But I agree you should stay far away from office jobs. Someone really would kill you with a stapler."

"And I'd deserve it." His knee was bouncing again. I decided to let it go. It kind of reminded me of one of the guys on my stepdad's crew, Liam, who did this thing where he sort of shook his hands out at the wrists, almost like jazz hands but down by his side. He called it "stimming," and it helped him calm down when he felt overwhelmed. Mick said Liam was the best painter he'd ever worked with, and it didn't cost him anything extra to make sure the rest of his crew were quiet and kept the music off while Liam worked to accommodate his issues with noise.

Thinking of Mick brought me back to my approaching gap year and how I might end up working for him again if I couldn't come up with anything else. Caleb's knee bouncing suddenly felt like a good idea. I considered trying it out myself, but he might think I was making fun of him.

"Speaking of not a desk job . . . " I remembered how Caleb's plan was to work at his parents' restaurants. "Do you like working at the restaurant?"

"Washing dishes isn't great," Caleb said. "But I like serving. And hosting."

I could imagine that. Caleb was such a people person.

"You don't get to cook, I guess," I said.

"Usually only in the food truck," Caleb said. "Though I'll get to do some this summer in the restaurant," he said. "But probably only on slow nights and with Aunt Zeina staring over my shoulder." He laughed. "She's my aunt and she's the chef. It's like a double whammy."

"I didn't know your parents had a food truck, too," I said.

"My parents started out of a food truck," he said. "When they first got to Canada." He smiled. "They still use it at festivals and stuff, with way fewer options on the menu. That's when I get to help out with the cooking, usually." He looked at me. "I like it, though. My oldest brother is even thinking he might try to launch his own business and use the truck full-time. If he does, I could help him. I just need to figure out if I like any of it enough to make it my whole thing, I guess."

I nodded.

"Other than drawing, what do you like doing?" Caleb said.

"Video games," I said, "which isn't a career."

"E-sports," Caleb said, holding up one hand.

I snorted.

"Maybe not," he said. "What else?"

"I like music, but I don't know how to play an instrument or anything," I said. "Raj makes these amazing playlists, and I could listen to them all day."

"Really?" Caleb said. "What kind of songs?"

"Well, I'd show you," I said, "but my phone — "

"Oh my God, Benny," Caleb said. He rolled his eyes, but he was smiling. "Let it go." He tilted his head. "Wait. Don't tell me. I bet you have 'Let It Go' on your phone, don't you?"

I did. It was a great song to listen to when I wanted

to tell the world to leave me alone. Elsa was 'Life Goals,' frankly. A rent-free ice castle on top of a mountain? Sign me up. "There's no way to know," I said.

"You do," Caleb said. He narrowed his eyes. "You're an Elsa."

"For the record," I said. "It's basically a gay anthem song. It's on every Pride playlist. 'Into the Unknown,' too."

He shook his head.

"It's from the sequel," I said. "*Panic! at the Disco* does a really great cover of it." I smiled. "I'd play it for you, but my phone — "

"Ugh!" Caleb threw his head back in his chair, and I laughed. He turned his head and smiled. I bet that smile got him good tips when he worked at the food truck, grinning down at people as he handed them their food.

Thinking of him at the food truck made me realize something. "Cooking," I said.

"Hrm?" he said.

"I like cooking," I said. "Mick and I cook dinner

most nights. He's really good, and my mom . . . " I waved a hand. "She's not bad at cooking or anything, but she always said she cooked because she has to feed us, but when Mick and her got together, he started teaching me things." I remembered the first time he'd told me nothing beat homemade pasta. We'd spent an entire Saturday making it, and it had been one of the best days ever. "I look up stuff online, and we try it out."

"Do you think you'd like cooking for people?" Caleb asked.

I blinked. "I don't know." But for the first time, my first thought wasn't nope.

"You should add it to your plan," Caleb said. "I could help. I mean, my parents would probably make you start on dishes, but like I said, there's the food truck at festivals and stuff."

"Really?" Wait. Was Caleb offering to help me get a job at his family restaurant? Because it sounded like that's what he was offering, and that would be *amazing*.

"Why not?" Caleb said. "I know you're not a slacker, my folks would love you, and you need a job."

He shrugged. "I mean, I can't promise anything, but I know they'll be hunting for people."

"Thank you," I said. I took a breath. "That . . . that would be *awesome*."

"It's no big deal," Caleb said. "Email me a resumé. I'll make sure they get it."

"Okay," I said. And then I had to stop talking because my throat felt like it was closing, and my chest was tight. I turned to stare back out the window again because for some reason, I felt like I was about to bawl my eyes out.

What was even happening?

09 Caleb Khoury Has Great Taste

THE RAIN GOT WORSE AND WORSE, and the train got slower and slower. Eventually, we were crawling along, barely moving at all. It was this long, flat, boring part of the trip, with nothing but fields to either side of us. The fields had really flooded outside the window, and when I looked down, the water was almost right up to the tracks.

"It's like *Spirited Away* out there," Caleb said.

I turned my head so fast I nearly gave myself

whiplash. He'd been leaning over to see out the window, too, but now he was staring at me, his brown eyes wide.

"What?" he said.

"You know *Spirited Away*?" I said. It was one of my favourite anime movies, about a girl who ends up in this spirit realm and has to rescue her parents, recover her name, and save a dragon. At one point, she takes a train running on tracks under the surface of a lake.

"Yeah," Caleb said. "It's pretty good."

I held up one hand. Caleb had done it again. He'd said something nice and then ruined it by saying something awful. "*Pretty good*? It's the best Miyazaki."

"Dude, no." Caleb shook his head. "*Princess Mononoke* is the best Miyazaki."

I stared at him. How could Caleb know Miyazaki movies but also be *so very wrong*? "But *Princess Mononoke* is so *gory*," I exclaimed.

"I said what I said." He crossed his arms, smiling his smug smile. He looked cool and confident, and I wanted to scream because he was *so annoying*. How was it possible to be so wrong?

"What about *Kiki's Delivery Service*?" I said, hoping he at least saw the genius of the little witch girl. It was a classic 'find your own way in the big city' story, but with magic and a talking cat named Jiji. Jiji is awesome.

"Meh," he said, shaking his head. "Now, *Nausicaä*? That one rocked."

"But *Kiki's Delivery Service* has Jiji!" It was possible I was getting way, way too into this conversation, but how dare he deny the snarkiest of little black cats?

"It also has pumpkin and herring pie." Caleb clearly wasn't going to budge on this.

"I can't believe you like Miyazaki movies and still manage to get it wrong," I said, crossing my own arms and staring right back. I probably didn't look half as cool and determined as he did, which was even more annoying.

"Wrong?" He snorted. "Oh, dude, no. I'm not the one who is wrong here. Next, you'll tell me you liked *The Wind Rises*."

"It's so good!" I was talking way too loud, I realized, and dropped my voice. "He found a way to reach his dreams despite not being able to fly. *Oh my God*, what is wrong with you?"

Caleb shook his head, then cracked a smile and laughed again. "You're too easy."

"What?" What did *that* mean?

"I like them all," he said, shrugging.

"You — " He liked them all? I dropped my arms, sighing.

He grinned.

"You're the worst," I said. Now I was grumpy. Again.

"*Princess Mononoke* is definitely my favourite, though," he said. He leaned back in his seat and rolled his head to the side to look at me, again. "But I can see why you like *Spirited Away* more."

I exhaled, deciding that was the closest thing I'd probably get from Caleb. He'd never admit his wrongness. How he could prefer running for his life while being chased by demons to riding a magical train across a lake was beyond me.

I had an idea. I could show him the train scene was better than anything in *Princess Mononoke*. I could draw a picture. Put him right in it. Except, as usual, the moment I had the idea I started second-guessing myself.

"What's wrong?" Caleb said. He was still watching me. One of his eyebrows rose, and he shifted to be more on his side in the chair, and his expression did it. I had to draw him. Caleb Khoury had a face that needed to be drawn.

"Don't move," I said.

"Where would I go, Benny?" he said.

"No, I mean, don't move in your chair," I said. I grabbed my backpack from in front of my feet and unzipped it, pulling out my sketchpad and a pencil. Then I turned to the side as much as I could in my own chair, looking at him and flipping open to a fresh page.

"Are you gonna draw me?" he asked. He was grinning, though, so I didn't *think* he thought I was a giant dork.

"I'm proving you wrong," I said.

"Huh?"

"Stay still," I said.

STUCK WITH YOU

I worked quickly, not letting myself get too caught up trying to make it perfect or anything. Drawing people in different anime styles was something I'd been working on for nearly two years now. Raj said I was good at it. They didn't say things that weren't true just to be nice. I took a few seconds to outline a bench. I didn't remember exactly what the train seats looked like in *Spirited Away* but that was okay. Then I set to work on an anime version of Caleb. I really looked at his face to notice the details. When I drew his eyes, I noticed he had strong eyebrows. They curved down to points and were a little tricky to translate to an anime style. I took a second to draw the dent in his chin, then added the faint dimples when he smiled. By the time I finished his short, slightly messy hair, I was in the zone. My pencil flew. My mind wasn't crowded with worries. Even though the train was rocking back and forth, the drawing was happening. I didn't overthink, and I didn't go into major detail anywhere else, either. I drew him in the clothes he was wearing. T-shirt, sweatpants, sneakers. Easy enough.

"Can I see?" Caleb asked.

"I haven't finished the background," I said. I'd only drawn a vague outline of the bench he was sitting on. It was barely a few lines. "But you're done, yeah." Except, suddenly, this felt like a *terrible* idea. Why had I done this? My picture of him on a train wouldn't change his mind about which movie was best.

But he might take one look and change his mind about me not being a total dork.

"So . . . let me see?" Caleb said, smiling and leaning forward. "Do you know how hard it is to sit still that long?"

"Five minutes?" I said.

"More like ten, and we already discussed this. Sitting still is torture," he said. He reached for my sketch pad, and I tugged it back.

"Dude," he said. "Come on." He grinned and held out his hand.

"Fine," I said. "But it's just a sketch. And like I said, the background isn't done yet." I took a breath and handed him my sketch pad.

"That looks like me." His eyes widened. "You're really good." He glanced over at me. "You seriously just did this, right now?"

"You watched me," I said. "And I'm glad you like it. See how he's on a train? Way cooler than running through the woods from a giant wolf demon."

"I don't think you can hear the words you're saying out loud," Caleb said, nudging my shoulder with one hand. "This is really cool. Can I have this? No one has ever drawn a picture of me before."

"Can I finish it, first?" I said. If he was going to keep it, I wasn't going to leave it half-done.

"Of course," he said, grinning. He was still holding it, though.

"Oh, wow, that's really good," came a voice from over my shoulder. I looked up. Cute Guy was back.

"Isn't it great?" Caleb said, holding it up to Cute Guy. "My friend Benny drew it," he pointed at me.

My friend Benny. Caleb surprised me. Were we friends? I tried not to dwell on all the different things I was feeling about the word and smiled at Cute Guy. Up close, his jacket was even cooler. Retro and leather, but he had all sorts of little patches and stuff sewn onto it. I spotted the little maple leaf done in a pride rainbow Caleb had seen.

"It's really good," Cute Guy said to me. He even nodded at me for a split second. Then he went right back to smiling at Caleb. I almost laughed because Cute Guy was *not* being subtle. My yelling about prom threesomes hadn't rattled Cute Guy as much as we'd thought.

"You mentioned you knew some good places to eat in Ottawa?" Cute Guy said.

"Yeah, I do," Caleb said. I imagined he was thinking of his parents' places.

"Here," Cute Guy said, pulling a phone from his pocket and handing it to him. "Put your number in. Then I can ask you for advice tomorrow."

Okay, Cute Guy definitely had confidence. I'd never make a direct move like that. Also, Cute Guy had nearly perfect teeth. A whole mouth of straight white teeth I'd have said had to be the work of braces, except he had a little gap between his front two. Somehow, the little gap made him cuter. Caleb cleared his throat and tapped on the guy's phone, handing it back. Cute Guy slid it into his pocket.

"Thanks," Cute Guy said. He aimed a really big smile at Caleb, then kept walking, heading to the back of the train and, I supposed, the bathroom.

Caleb turned and stared at me, his eyes wide. I couldn't decide if he was panicked or impressed. Maybe it was both?

"Did that just happen?" he asked.

"Oh, come on." I snorted. "I've seen that happen to you before." With girls, sure, but still.

Caleb shook his head but didn't say anything. I reached over and took the drawing back from him. "You want me to add Cute Guy in the seat beside you?" I teased. "I could draw little hearts above his head, and give you panic sweats."

"Do not," he said, shaking his head. He frowned. "Did I look panicked?"

"No, not really," I said, because it was true. "You looked fine. You *always* look fine."

"Was that a compliment?" He leaned back away from me. "Benny, I'm shocked."

I rolled my eyes. "I was just trying to make you feel better." The truth was, watching Cute Guy flirt with Caleb had left me feeling off balance, and I wasn't sure why. I mean, until today I hadn't known Caleb would flirt with a guy, but it wasn't that.

Probably it had more to do with Cute Guy's complete lack of interest in me. He gave Caleb his number. Being jealous of Caleb wasn't exactly the greatest feeling in the world. It didn't help Caleb had only talked to Cute Guy because of me. I'd dared him to do it.

This was silly. Being jealous of Caleb was silly. When it came to guys, I was the one with experience, not him. I mean, mostly my experience was limited to making out with a guy at queer camp last year, some mostly naked groping with one of Ethan's friends when I stayed overnight at a party Ethan threw over Christmas Break, and both of those guys had kind of fizzled out thanks to distance.

I considered the drawing of Caleb, wondering what to add.

"You should put yourself in the seat beside me." Caleb tapped the empty spot beside the anime version of himself on the paper. "You can call it 'Me and the Jerk Who Broke My Phone, Who Always Looks Fine.'"

I laughed. "Uh-huh."

"I'm serious, though," he said. "Pop yourself there." He tapped the page again. "In honour of how long this train ride has been."

I faced him. He was serious. "I don't really draw myself," I said. When I did stuff like this, I used my friends. Mostly Raj. Or I'd find photos of people if I wanted to try different faces or hairstyles or whatever.

"Why not? You don't know what you look like?" Caleb said.

"Kind of," I said, because that really was the thing. "I usually look at people when I draw them."

Caleb pulled out his phone, unlocked it, and held it up. "Don't move," he said.

I froze.

"Okay, but maybe don't look like you need to poop."

I laughed, and he took a photo. He tapped on the screen again and smiled. "There," he said, handing me the phone.

I braced myself, then looked at the photo. I usually cringe at pictures of myself. This one was good, though. My hair wasn't too bad. I was laughing. My eyes weren't closed. The more I looked, the more I was pretty sure it was one of the best pictures of me ever taken. The guy in the photo was happy and relaxed. The guy in the photo was having fun.

He was *comfortable*.

Huh.

10 Caleb Khoury Is So Annoying

FOR THE RECORD, drawing yourself is weird. Drawing yourself while someone else watches is even weirder. When the someone else is Caleb Khoury? It goes beyond weird and into bizarre because, apparently, when Caleb watches someone draw, he makes noises.

As I worked on adding myself in beside Caleb in the picture, I kept track of his noises.

First was a little hum. Kind of a "Hm, that was interesting" noise. He hummed when I drew the little lines for my glasses and when I outlined the shadows behind us on the seat. I'd eventually crosshatch to make the shadows.

His second noise was little puffs of air he exhaled through his nose. I was pretty sure those meant he thought something was funny, because he puffed when I checked my feet to look at my shoes, which obviously weren't in the photo. He also puffed when I put a little box between us and drew in a bunch of cookies, granola bars, and bananas.

The third noise he made was more like the sound he'd made when he was texting Emma: a grunt. Those he saved for when I erased something. The third time he did it, I looked up at him.

"What?" he said.

"Something wrong?" I asked.

"The hand you drew was fine," Caleb said. "I don't know why you erased it."

I'd erased my hand because hands were tricky and I'd wanted to put myself holding a cup of tea, and I hadn't quite gotten the angle right. I raised one eyebrow, staring at him. "Which one of us has done this before?"

"Fine, fine," he said. His lips twitched. He was fighting off a smile. "You're right."

Once I was done with the tea, I tackled the worst thing: my hair. I went back to the photo, tapping Caleb's phone screen to wake it back up.

A text popped up. It wasn't from Emma. It was from "Dad."

You okay to take the bus home? It's going to be late, and I need to be at the restaurant.

I handed the phone to Caleb, who tilted his head. "All done?"

"You got a text from your dad," I said.

"Oh." He read it. Then he exhaled little puff of air through his nose and typed in a response to his dad's text. He waited for a reply. When it came, he did another puff through his nose, and then took a deep breath and tapped on the phone, putting it back in front of me once he had the picture of me back on the screen.

"Did your dad tell a joke?"

Caleb glanced at me. "What? No." He had the little line between his eyebrows again.

"You thought something was funny, though," I said.

"Not funny so much as typical." Caleb shrugged. His gaze went back to the drawing. "You're so fast."

"Lots of practise." I glanced at the photo and decided to just go for it with the drawing of my hair. If it looked messy it would be more realistic, anyway. I started with the little "poof" thing my hair does at the front that always, always went to one side more than the other, then glanced at him. "What was typical?" I said, going back to the drawing. "With your dad, I mean?"

"He asked me if I'd happened to bring my bus pass with me," Caleb said, then snorted. "Like I'd leave without it."

"Okay," I said.

"I kind of assumed he'd end up not picking me up," Caleb said.

"Ah," I said, getting it now. He'd mentioned before the only bad thing he could think of about his parents

STUCK WITH YOU

was how busy they were. "Is it a long ride?" I had no idea where he lived, but the train station was at least on the Transitway.

"Not really," Caleb said, shrugging again. He leaned over the drawing. "That really looks like us."

"And it's done," I said, putting down my pencil. It wasn't a bad job, either, if I did say so myself. Cartoon Caleb was sort of leaning on his seat, all cool and relaxed, but I'd drawn myself looking . . . well, grumpy with him, staring at him over the tea I was drinking with thick, angry eyebrows over my glasses.

"And clearly you're still mad at me," Caleb said, noting my little counterpart's expression.

"Cartoon me holds a grudge," I nodded.

"Does that mean the real you doesn't?" Caleb said.

"I think five hours on a train is long enough," I said. "It's time to let it go."

"Especially when it was only supposed to be four hours and change," Caleb said, stretching in his seat and making his shoulders pop.

I winced, and he laughed.

"It feels good," he said.

"If you say so." It still sounded awful.

Caleb tapped the corner of the paper. "Sign it," he said. I felt a little silly, but I scribbled down my initials and then tore the paper out of my sketchbook and handed it to him.

To my surprise, Caleb held it carefully, then pulled a book out of his backpack and slid my drawing inside the front cover. It shouldn't have made me feel good that he didn't want it to get wrinkled, but it did.

I swallowed. Then I took a deep breath. I had this shaky feeling in my stomach I didn't want to think about. I hadn't had this feeling often. In fact, the last time had been Ethan's party last Christmas, and . . .

"You okay?" he asked.

"I'm fine."

"That was a big sigh for someone who's fine," Caleb said. "And I bet you don't normally admit when you're not fine, either, do you? You really try not to bother people at all, don't you?" He crossed his arms, grinning again. "Except for me."

Oh sure. *Now* Caleb gets insightful. Where was this when he was throwing basketballs around the school hallway?

"It's nothing," I said, because I sure as heck wasn't going to say what I was really thinking.

When Caleb frowned, I decided he wasn't going to stop unless I came up with something, so I went with the first thing I could think of.

"Your dad cancelling made me wonder if my stepdad would still be there," I said. It was true, to a point. I had wondered for a moment if Mick would be there, but like Caleb, I had my bus pass, so if Mick couldn't stick around, it wouldn't be the end of the world.

"Oh," Caleb said, and he kind of flinched. "And you can't call or text him to check because . . . " He opened his hands and flicked his fingers in a 'hit me with it' way.

"Oh, you know why," I said. I narrowed my eyes, then laughed. "But like I said, cartoon me holds the grudge now. I gave it to him."

Caleb held out his phone. "If you want to call him . . . "

I almost took the phone, and then I stopped.

"What?" Caleb said.

"I don't remember his number." I tried to remember Mick's number, but the more I thought about it, the more I wasn't even sure I'd ever had it memorized in the first place.

"Isn't it, like, written on the side of his truck?" Caleb smirked.

It was. "Shut up," I said, annoyed. "Wow. This is pathetic."

"Your mom, then?" Caleb asked.

"It's fine," I said, shaking my head.

"You don't know her number, either?" Caleb said.

"How many phone numbers do *you* have memorized?" I said, not answering the question.

"You don't, do you?" He looked like he was trying not to burst out laughing.

"It's been a long day," I said.

He did laugh this time and shook his head. Then he rolled to the side to look at me. "I don't have the slightest idea what my dad's phone number is," he said.

Then his lips curled up in a smug smile. "But I know my mom's."

"You're so annoying," I said, which only made him laugh again.

Outside, the sun was going down, not that you could see much with the rain. The only thing I could see out the window was my own reflection, and behind me, Caleb's reflection, too. He'd sat back in his seat again, leaning back, and closed his eyes.

He was so good-looking. And funny. And kinder than I thought he'd be. The way he wanted to include Scott in his Prom, or how he'd agreed to talk to Donovan about how he spoke to Raj. And, oh yeah, also it turned out Caleb Khoury *did* like guys. And Cute Guy was definitely liking Caleb.

Which, well . . . wasn't a huge surprise. They were both so good-looking. I could easily see Caleb and Cute Guy hanging out and having fun. Going to one of Caleb's family restaurants together, for example. I had no doubt Cute Guy was angling for that. And they'd have a great time. Caleb was funny. Eating a meal with Caleb was fun, which I knew. In fact, hanging out with Caleb in any situation was fun, and made the time fly by, even when you were on a train going slow because of the weather.

I could only imagine how much fun it would be to hang out with Caleb on a real date. To have a restaurant meal together, and then maybe take a walk and get dessert somewhere else, like ice cream or something. He'd definitely do something silly — like smear ice cream on his chin and see how long it took his date to notice. And then maybe pretend he didn't understand until the date kissed it off.

Ugh. I closed my eyes and leaned back in my chair. I took a couple of breaths but made sure I didn't let out another big sigh. I didn't need to come up with another excuse for Caleb as to why I was sitting here feeling like a complete loser.

There was no excuse.

And boy was I ever a loser.

Because I wasn't picturing Cute Guy kissing the ice cream off Caleb Khoury's face on an imaginary date. I was picturing me.

Somehow, in the space of one train ride, I'd totally gotten a crush on Caleb Khoury.

11 Caleb Khoury Notices Things

I DIDN'T OPEN MY EYES AGAIN until we stopped at Fallowfield, which was the second-last stop and meant we were almost home. When I sat up again, Caleb pulled out his earbuds, slipped them into his case and slid his phone back into his pocket.

"Almost home," he said.

"Yep." I stretched, putting both arms over my head and leaning forward. Nothing popped, but it felt good.

"Did you have a good nap?" Caleb asked.

"Not bad," I lied. I hadn't slept at all. I forced myself to smile, even.

He frowned. "You okay?"

Okay, why could I not bluff this guy? I shook my head. "It's just been a long day."

"Tell me about it," Caleb said. "We were supposed to be home nearly an hour ago." He chuckled, then rolled his head on the back of his seat to face me. "I normally go stir-crazy on the train as it is. If I'd have been beside a stranger, this would have been a nightmare."

I laughed. Partly, it was funny because he said it so seriously, like having to be quiet and not talk was physically painful for him. But what was really funny was until we'd gotten on this train, I'd have called us strangers.

"I'm serious," he said. "I — "

His phone pinged.

He sighed and pulled it out of his pocket, read it, and groaned, throwing his head back.

"Let me guess," I said. "Emma?"

"She is not letting this go," he said, thudding his

head against the back of his chair. "She says I owe her the rental car."

"That makes zero sense," I said, shaking my head. "You don't owe her. She's the one who dumped you."

"Ouch, dude," Caleb said, putting a hand to his chest and smiling.

Okay, so maybe not the nicest way to put it.

"You know what I mean." I shook my head. It was easy to be annoyed at Emma on Caleb's behalf. She'd been awful to him. And, fine, I preferred it when he smiled, because I'd completely lost my mind and liked looking at his smile. And his arms. I forced my eyes back up to his face, though really, it didn't stop me from feeling tongue-tied and awkward. "Besides. You're taking Scott, as *friends*." Why did I emphasize that? Now Caleb was staring at me funny. Damn it. "And maybe Jasmine and Roy, if I crash and burn with the club."

"Is that what has you all jumpy?" Caleb eyed me. "You think you'll crash and burn with your friends?"

"I'm not good at confrontation," I said. It was true.

And if he thought *that* was why I was jumpy, it was fine by me. It felt sad and pathetic to say it out loud, though. It felt like I was admitting I was a coward. "I tend to try and make everyone feel better, but I don't think that's going to work for this."

"Oh, sure." Caleb laughed, shaking his head. "Tell me another one."

"What?" I said.

"You've been confronting me the whole train ride, Benny." He leaned back away from me. "And you definitely weren't trying to make me feel better. I think you've got this."

"I — " I started to argue, but the thing was, he wasn't wrong. I had been talking bluntly with Caleb the whole train ride. But it was *different*. "Yeah, but when you sat beside me, I was still mad at you. And I mean, you're *you*. I'm me. It didn't matter what you thought of me."

Caleb winced. "Yeah, you're brutal, Benny."

"No," I said. "No, you don't get it. I mean . . . We're very different. You move in a completely different circle than me. It wouldn't change anything. But I don't think that now. You're . . . " I closed my mouth because I had no idea how to say I thought he was actually a really nice guy, and I cared what he thought about me.

A lot. I cared a lot.

He raised one eyebrow.

"Anyway," I said. "It's different with the Rainbow Club. They're my entire circle of friends."

"Well," Caleb said, taking a deep breath, then chuckling. "Be mad at them, I guess."

"What?" I stared at him.

"Be mad. You said they were being awful, right?" Caleb asked.

I nodded. "They are. Yeah."

"I'm not saying you should, like, rage at them or anything, but . . . " He shrugged one shoulder. "They're being jerks. Treat them like jerks. You know how to put someone in their place. Trust me. I've experienced it." He grinned at me.

"You know who else is being a jerk?" I stared at him for a couple of seconds. "Emma is being a jerk."

He swallowed, then held out his hand. I blinked for a second. "We still got a deal?" he said.

I took his hand and shook it. And this time, he didn't let go right away. He sort of squeezed, and I'm pretty sure my entire body started sweating. When he finally let go, my hand was shaking.

"Deal," I said, clearing my throat.

Caleb pulled his phone out and typed for a bit. He showed me the screen.

I'm not giving you the car. I paid for it. I'm still going. With friends. You broke up with me. Please stop texting me about this.

When I finished reading, I looked at him. He was biting his bottom lip, and his dark eyes flicked back-and-forth. "It's not mean, right?" he said. "I'm not giving her the car, but I don't want to be cruel."

I *loved* that he didn't want to be cruel.

"It's not cruel," I said. "It's fair. And it's true."

He tapped the send button and it whooshed away. Then he pressed the power button until his phone turned off and put it back in his pocket. Then he frowned. "I need your number," he said, fishing it back out again.

"What?" I said.

"I want to know how it goes with your friends." He was powering his phone back on. "So, I can ask Jasmine and Roy to come with me if your friends turn out to suck." He handed it to me. "Be quick. I kind of want to turn it back off again before she replies."

I added myself to his contacts as fast as my shaky fingers could handle because holy crap, I was giving Caleb Khoury my number. "But you told her not to text you back."

He snorted. And sure enough, just as I was saving myself as a new contact on his phone, a reply popped up from Emma with the telltale ping noise. I looked away before I could read more than the first few words, which were bad enough.

You can't be serious right now!!! You can't —

"Crap," Caleb said, watching my face to see my reaction.

I pressed the power button on his phone until it shut off, then held it out to him. "So, I'd maybe not read it until tomorrow," I said. "She's not happy."

He groaned. "Oh, tomorrow is going to suck *so much*."

I was still trying to think of something to make him feel better when the speakers above us announced we were going to be arriving shortly in Ottawa at our final destination.

"At least we're finally home?" I said.

He laughed, rolling his head to the side. "Bright-side Benny for the win."

The first time he'd called me Benny I hadn't known whether I liked it or not. Now I knew. I did like it.

In fact, I liked it way too much.

The train pulled into the station a little while later, and you could tell everyone still on the train was beyond ready to get off. They all stood up, and it took us a little while to shuffle out the door with our bags and head into the tunnel that took us into the Ottawa train station. Caleb kept pace with me, but we walked in silence and took the escalator instead of the ramp once we got to the end of the tunnel. By the time we got to the top, quite a few people were already meeting up with the folks who'd come to get them, and we sort of spilled out into the milling crowd.

"Hey, Caleb?"

We both turned, and saw Cute Guy approaching, a big smile on his face, and his gaze entirely for Caleb.

I knew when I was beat. I stepped back to give them some space to talk and scanned the crowd. Finding a very tall red-haired construction worker with a beard is never a difficult job, and I spotted my stepdad a few seconds later. Mick was leaning against one of the pillars, hands in his pockets, watching the crowd.

He spotted me and smiled. I waved and started heading for him.

He met me halfway. "You made it," he said, smiling, and tugging me in with one arm for a quick hug and a pat on the back. "That must have been a long ride."

"It was," I said. "But I had someone to talk to. Thank you for waiting. I could have taken the bus."

"No." Mick shook his head, like that was silly.

"Who were you talking to?" he asked. "I thought your phone broke. Did your dad get you a new one?"

"Oh, um, no." I shook my head and then turned to point at Caleb and Cute Guy, only now it was only Caleb standing there. "Caleb Khoury," I said, pointing. "He goes to school with me."

"Ah," Mick said.

"Actually, Mick," I said, glancing back at him. "His dad couldn't wait for the train. He works at a restaurant. Owns it, actually. Could we maybe give him a ride so he doesn't have to take the bus in the rain?"

"Of course," Mick said, nodding. He rubbed his chin, smiling in a way that made me feel like he was trying not to laugh at me or something.

"Great, thanks." Was I blushing? I felt like I was blushing. I turned back to Caleb, and he happened to be looking at me, so I waved him over. He lifted his bag onto his shoulder and came up to us.

"We can give you a ride," I said.

"Oh, wow," Caleb said, turning to Mick. "Thank you so much. I'm not far from here."

"It's really no problem," Mick said. "Come on."

Mick led the way to the parking lot. He must have already used the machine to get the ticket to leave. Caleb and I trailed behind him for a few steps until we picked up the pace. Mick only had one speed, and it was 'very tall man with long legs' fast.

"Did you settle on a restaurant?" The moment I said it, I wished I hadn't.

"What?" Caleb glanced at me.

"Cute Guy," I said. "Did he ask you out to eat?" I tried to sound casual, but the truth was I didn't even want to know. Not really. Still, I managed to keep my voice almost normal.

"Yeah," Caleb looked down for a second. "He asked. But I . . . I said no."

We stepped out into the rain. Mick started moving even faster, and we sped up to keep up with him. It sort of cut off the conversation, and I wouldn't have known what to say, anyway, because I hadn't expected that.

Caleb turned Cute Guy down? *Why*?

Mick unlocked the truck, and I opened the door.

"I'll take the back," I said, sliding into the much smaller space behind the front seats, "so you can tell Mick how to get to your house."

By the time I had my seatbelt on, I realized I'd been thinking about Caleb and Cute Guy the wrong way. I'd been wondering what I would do if someone like Cute Guy had asked me out.

And that was simple. I'd have said yes, probably embarrassing myself somehow, but I'd have been over the moon.

But Caleb Khoury wasn't me. He'd had a girlfriend until last week. This was brand new to him, and I remembered what he'd said before, how it felt different. And I'd agreed. It was different. It was also what I was used to. But he wasn't.

Caleb Khoury had never gone on a date with a guy before.

And, clearly, he didn't want to.

12 Caleb Khoury Doesn't Mind the Rain

MICK ASKED CALEB for his address, and it turned out Caleb was right. It wasn't far at all.

"Thank you, again," Caleb said.

"It's really no trouble," Mick said. "In fact, it's on our way."

"My dad had to go to work," Caleb said.

"Ben mentioned he owns a restaurant?" Mick said.

"Yeah," Caleb glanced at me. "My parents have two of them. Khoury's in the Market, and Big K

Shawarma on Bank."

"Your parents run Big K?" Mick said, and I could tell he was doing his biggest smile just from the sound of his voice. "My whole team loves Big K. Any time we've got a project anywhere near the Glebe, that's our lunch of choice. So good." He glanced at me in the rear-view mirror. "Didn't your mom get us reservations at Khoury's once, too, Ben?"

I nodded. "For her birthday, two years ago."

"Right, right." Mick nodded. He turned his attention back to the road. "It was really good. My daughters even liked it, and they were at that age when all they wanted was chicken nuggets." Mick patted the steering wheel. "That was a huge win."

Caleb laughed. "I'll tell my folks. And my aunt. She's the head chef at Khoury's. I'll let her know she outdid chicken nuggets."

Okay, I was starting to see what Caleb meant by how parents liked him. He was talking so effortlessly with Mick, and he'd known him for five minutes, and was making my stepdad laugh. It should be annoying, but it wasn't.

"That's my house up there," Caleb said, pointing. "The grey one with the white door."

I couldn't help checking out where he lived. It was a nice enough house, had a small yard in front of it, but looked more or less like all the other houses on the street, the way so much of Ottawa did. I wasn't sure what I'd been expecting, like maybe Caleb's house should stand out like he did, but it didn't.

Mick pulled into the driveway, and Caleb thanked him again, then the two of us hopped out so Caleb could go home, and I could get into the front seat where my legs fit better.

"Thank you," Caleb said, just sort of standing there in the rain in his driveway. It wasn't pouring anymore. It was more like a light shower, but he was still getting wet.

"It's fine," I said. I was also standing there in the rain in his driveway, getting wet.

"I should go inside before a giant furry monster with an umbrella shows up," Caleb said.

"Yeah." I laughed. It was another Miyazaki movie reference. "Or a cat bus."

"A cat bus would be cool." Caleb didn't move. "Don't forget to send me your resumé," he said. "For the restaurant?"

"Right," I said. "Right." And then, because apparently my mouth couldn't come up with anything else to say, I said "right" a third time. Why was I like this?

He nodded. "Okay. Thanks again. Let me know how it goes with your friends."

I nodded back, if only because I didn't want to say "right" again.

"Night, Benny," he said, and he backed away.

"Good night," I said.

I climbed into the truck and closed the door. Caleb waved from his front door, and Mick did his usual thing of waiting until Caleb got his key in and the door opened before he pulled back out of the driveway again.

Once we were back on the road, Mick asked, "Did he ask you for a resumé?"

I hadn't realized Mick was listening. I turned to

him. "Is that okay?" I asked. "I really appreciate you making room for me at work, but Caleb said they're looking for people at his family restaurants. Probably washing dishes and doing tables, but sometimes working in their food truck. I like cooking. I thought it might be a good way to find out if I like it enough. You know, to maybe do it for more than just for fun?"

Mick smiled, though he didn't look at me. "Sounds like a great idea," he said. "You're a good cook."

"Because you taught me," I said.

"You teach yourself, too," Mick said. "We watch those videos together, and I've never made half those things either."

I nodded, feeling a bit relieved. "You're sure it's okay if I get a different job for my gap year?"

"Ben, I want you to try new things," Mick said. "I mean, I'll miss having you around, but I don't think either of us thought you were going into my business, did we?" He glanced over for a second before turning his gaze back to the road.

"No," I said, and it felt kind of nice to say it out

loud. "I guess not." He wasn't making me feel bad about it or acting worried. "Though I'm still good for helping at home. I like learning how everything works."

"Good." Mick smiled another one of his big-beard smiles. "Everyone should know how to replace a light switch or shut off the water and replace a toilet." He tapped the steering wheel. "In fact, this winter it'll be time to tackle the spare bathroom."

"Okay," I said. I knew both Mick and my mom didn't like nearly anything about the small bathroom on the ground floor of our house. Apparently, I would be learning how to replace bathroom fixtures this winter, which was cool enough.

We drove in silence for a while.

"So," Mick said.

My stepdad has about a dozen different ways of saying "so." There's the 'bad news' way, which is the total worst because he hates letting people down. There's a 'good news' way, too, where I know I'm in for a long and rambling talk. He likes making us all impatient for him to finally spill whatever awesome news it might be. Usually, it's my mom who tells him to spit it out.

But this "so" wasn't one I'd heard before. It wasn't a 'good news' one or a 'bad news' one or even a 'let's chat' one. If I had to choose, I'd say this new "so" was maybe *nervous*?

Which was weird. Mick didn't really do nervous.

"What's up?" I looked at him. He glanced at me before aiming his eyes back on the road.

"Caleb seems nice," he said.

"He is," I said. Mick didn't say anything else, and the silence started to feel weird again, so I admitted the truth. "I didn't really think so before today."

"Hm," Mick said. That was another noise he could make mean dozens of different things. "Good train trip, then? Even with the delay?"

"It was," I said. I took a breath, and then I admitted something else. "Better than Toronto."

"Did it not go well with your dad?" Mick said. Now he was using his 'problem customer' voice. That voice came out a lot on his phone. It made me wonder if he thought my father might be a problem customer.

I thought about how to answer what he'd asked me. *Did it not go well with your dad?* It was a big question. It sounded simple enough, but wasn't.

"It was okay," I said, but it felt too much like a lie. "I mean, it was the usual."

Mick sighed. "I'm sorry."

"He didn't even *try* to help me get a new phone," I said. "He said it would be easier for mom to do it because I'm on her plan, but . . . " I took a breath. "Honestly? I think he just didn't want to."

Mick sighed again. He had this thing where if he couldn't think of something good to say then he didn't say anything. After a few seconds, he said, "That means you didn't get to text with Raj or anyone while you were there?"

"Right," I said. It was almost funny that he was sympathizing with me about my phone. On a regular basis, Mick told my sisters and I that we spent way too much time on our phones. But he understood.

"I'm sorry," he said, again. "We'll get it fixed after school on Monday."

I bit my lip. I remembered what Caleb had said on the train when we were talking about our parents, and I'd admitted I was glad I only had a few more trips to Toronto ahead of me. *Have you told your mom you don't like it?* "Can I be honest?"

"Of course," Mick said, and he glanced at me again. He seemed surprised. I couldn't tell why, exactly.

"I'd rather not go at all," I said. "To Toronto. But I know I have to, and I don't want to make waves. He doesn't really get me, and it's not like it's terrible. He's not mean or anything. It's just . . . " I took a breath. I felt a little sick. Maybe this was a mistake. "I guess I'm glad this was my last March Break in Toronto."

We pulled up to a red traffic light. Mick faced me, and now he looked sad rather than surprised. "Ben, these trips are always up to you, okay?"

"But I have to spend three weeks with him, don't I?" I asked. I was pretty sure that was the deal.

"Well," Mick said, "you let us deal with that." He just looked at me for a second. "How long have you felt like this? About Toronto, and visiting your dad?"

I took a deep breath, and honestly, it was embarrassing, but I was suddenly very close to crying. I think Mick could tell, because he didn't make me say anything.

"Oh, Ben," he said. "It's okay. If you don't want to go this summer, your mom and I will talk to your dad, and we'll all figure something out together, okay?"

The light changed, and we started moving again.

13 Caleb Khoury Flexes a Lot

MICK LET THINGS GET QUIET AGAIN for a while, which was good. I took a few minutes, just sort of breathing and watching the wipers swipe the rain off the windshield. I couldn't believe I'd told him I didn't want to see my father. It wasn't like me. I didn't do stuff like this.

"You know you can talk to me about anything, right?" Mick said. "When something's bothering you?"

Apparently, I'd surprised Mick as much as I'd surprised myself.

"I know," I said. And I think I did. Mick was amazing. "I guess I just . . . " I wasn't sure how to finish the sentence without sounding sad.

"Didn't want to make waves?" Mick asked.

I sighed. "Yeah. Raj says I do that too much."

"I like Raj," Mick said. It was a nice way to say he agreed.

"Caleb thought Raj and I were dating," I said. I wasn't sure why I said it.

"I can see how people might think that," Mick said.

We drove in silence for a few seconds.

"So," Mick said again, and this time it was definitely Mick's 'teasing' version of the word. "Are you going to ask Caleb out?"

"Huh?" I choked. "No. I . . . *What*? Caleb? Why would you ask that?"

"Ben." Mick laughed, glancing at me again. "I know what it looks like when you have a crush."

I groaned. This was the worst. The absolute worst. I managed not to die on the spot and sank down deep into my seat. "Really? You could tell?"

"Yes." Mick sounded like he was trying not to laugh again. "I could."

"Oh God," I said, because something awful had occurred to me. "Do you think Caleb could tell?"

"I don't know." Mick didn't laugh again, which was good. "I think most people don't realize when someone has a crush on them."

"Thank God," I said. I thought about how often I'd looked at Caleb's arms. Why had I done that so often? Because they were great arms.

Great arms attached to a great guy. Caleb seemed to be a great guy.

Oh man. I groaned again.

"I really don't think he knows," Mick said. I didn't think Mick was trying to make me feel better. I think he really believed it. He had that in common with Raj. Mick didn't say stuff unless he meant it. "Which is why you should ask him out."

Me? Asking out Caleb? I tried to imagine it, but I couldn't. "But I'm a train," I said.

"What?" Mick exclaimed with a little laugh.

"You're a *train*?"

"It's a metaphor," I said. "If people were cars and planes and stuff. I'm a train. I stay on the rails." I needed Mick to understand how different Caleb and I were. "I go to the same places. And I'm happy. I like being in places I already know. But Caleb? He's . . . I don't know. Caleb's, like, a hot air balloon. Or maybe a dirt bike?" I took a breath. "You get what I mean?"

"You're different," Mick said.

"Right."

"But that doesn't mean you can't complement each other."

We stopped at another light, and Mick looked at me. "Tell me something, Ben," Mick said, putting his hand on my shoulder and squeezing. "Was this the first time you two hung out?"

"Yeah," I said, not sure why it mattered.

"So, you and Caleb have been together on a train ride. Once." Mick tilted his head. "We both heard him brush off someone you both called 'Cute Guy.'"

"Oh my God," I said, putting a hand over my eyes.

"How did you even hear that?" He'd been walking ahead of us.

"I have dad ears." Mick patted out a little beat on the steering wheel and laughed. "But that's not all. When we dropped Caleb off, he acted like someone who didn't want his day to end. He stood out in the rain to say goodbye, kept talking to you, asked you to text him . . . " Mick raised his eyebrows. "You know how I said most people don't realize when someone has a crush on them? Read the signs, son."

The light changed, and Mick started driving again.

No. *No way.*

I didn't say anything until we pulled into the driveway. I'd been so ready to get home all day, but now I just sat there in the truck. My head felt too full. Mick couldn't be right. He *couldn't* be. Caleb brushed off Cute Guy because Caleb wasn't ready for the drama of being out and dating another guy while he was in high school. He'd pretty much said so.

Right?

Except, no. No, he'd said he hadn't wanted to

come out while he was dating *Emma*. That wasn't the same thing at all.

And he *had* brushed off Cute Guy.

Because he doesn't want to date a guy.

Or . . .

Or because he didn't want to date *Cute Guy*?

My stepdad seemed to notice I wasn't quite ready to go inside, because he turned off the truck and didn't move, either.

Okay. Let's pretend the world was upside down and Caleb *would* be willing to go on a date with a guy. With me. Then what? It didn't change anything because . . .

"I've never asked anyone out," I said. At queer camp, at Ethan's party, I'd always been the one asked. Not because I was such a hot ticket or anything, but because approaching someone was terrifying. I needed someone to flirt with me before I even considered flirting back.

"Oof. Yeah. That part is rough. I never did, either," Mick said, facing me. "I was always too shy."

I stared at him, stunned. Mick? *Mick* was too shy? Big bearded Mick? If someone like my stepdad couldn't ask people out, I was *doomed.*

"But wait," I said. "You and mom . . . "

"She made the first move," Mick said, chuckling.

"Mom?" I sort of choked on the word.

"Do you know what she did?" Mick asked.

Did I *want* to know? I couldn't decide. I mean, this was my mom and my stepdad. Ew. But also, I was feeling kind of desperate here, so . . . "No," I said. "What did she do?"

I hoped this wasn't too gross. Please let this not be gross.

"She just asked," Mick said.

I exhaled, relieved. Not gross. Not helpful, either, but not gross.

"She told me she liked how I treated her when I did her renovation," Mick said. "Listening to her, and how I spoke to her. And she wanted to know if I would treat her the same way on a date."

"Oh." I blinked. Wow. "Mom was smooth?" I said.

"Your mom is the smoothest," Mick said, smiling again. "I bet it runs in the family." He reached out and rubbed my head, messing up my hair the way he'd done when he'd first married my mom. He hadn't done it in a while. It made me smile back at him.

Me. Smooth. Ha.

We finally got out of the truck, splashing through some rainy slush to get inside. My sisters were already in bed, but my mom had stayed up to give me a welcome-home hug, and I had a shower. Once I was ready for bed, though, I instead went to my computer and found my resumé, but when I went to send it to Caleb, I realized I didn't have his email address. I didn't imagine he'd have it posted on his social media, but I went and checked, anyway. Caleb Khoury's photo feed had a lot of pictures of him flexing his biceps. Apparently, whenever his friends took group shots, flexing was his go-to move. It was sort of goofy and definitely made him look like a show-off, but somehow it worked for him.

I suppose if I had arms like his I'd show them off, too.

When I scrolled back far enough to get back to warm weather, I learned he did the bicep flex when he wasn't wearing a shirt, too, which was an even better look on him. He had a really nice chest, too. Thankfully, he didn't have a six-pack, or I wouldn't have had the courage to do the next thing, which was to send him a direct message asking for his email so I could send him my resumé.

I waited for a few minutes in case he responded.

Okay, fine, I scrolled his shirtless photos for a while. The guy posted a lot of them over the summer. There was a wide variety. Caleb by his family's pool. Caleb in his family's pool. Caleb with Scott, Roy, Donovan, and the rest of the basketball team in the pool.

He really liked the pool, apparently.

I noticed Emma never seemed to actually get in the water in any of the summer photos. She was always on one of the chairs beside the pool, usually with her friends, all of whom were perfectly posed, too. She was really pretty. They all were.

Caleb didn't respond, and I remembered he'd

turned off his phone after that last text with Emma. Maybe he was taking my advice to not turn it back on until tomorrow. Which reminded me, tomorrow I'd agreed to try and talk to everyone about asking Jasmine and Roy to join us for Prom.

My stomach twisted up into a knot. Then I yawned. Who knew you could be anxious and tired? Also, it made no sense. All I'd done today was sit on a train, and somehow, I was exhausted. I closed my computer and went to bed.

When I finally got under my blanket, I ended up staring at my ceiling, my head spinning about dozens of things.

Okay, fine, my head was spinning about one thing. One person.

Maybe what I needed was to get my train off the rails? Be more like Scott and Roy and the other people Caleb hung out with? But no. That didn't feel right. For one, my life wasn't a movie. I wasn't about to meet up with Raj and Lin and Ethan for a makeover and show up at school on Monday suddenly cool enough to ask out Caleb Khoury. I was a train, and I wasn't going to turn into a hot air balloon.

What had Caleb said about trains?

Some trains are exciting. Bullet trains. They go, like, hundreds of kilometres an hour.

Hundreds of kilometres an hour wasn't my speed either.

But . . .

But maybe I could speed up.

At least a little.

I closed my eyes, and finally fell asleep.

14 Caleb Khoury Shook On It

MONDAY MORNING, I spotted most of the Rainbow Club in the usual spot in the hallway by the library, where we always gathered before heading to our homerooms. Jasmine wasn't there, again, and I remembered my double-handshake deal with Caleb and took a deep breath.

I could do this. Raj and Lin were talking. Raj had their usual hoodie-and-jeans combo going on, though I noticed they'd had their fade redone over the break.

Lin was apparently in the mood for red today, with a kind of flowy, loose red blouse over her jeans, red kicks, and red fingernails and lipstick to match. Beside them, Grayson and Ethan were apparently having a thumb war. Grayson was wearing his favourite T-shirt again: 'Real Men Kiss Men.' I didn't always get Grayson. He sometimes seemed to want people to be angry with him, and sort of put it all out there like he was spoiling for a fight, but I did wish I was half as brave as him. Ethan, on the other hand, looked catwalk ready in a pair of shiny grey pants, a sky-blue button-down, and his rimless glasses. Jessica, in her usual ensemble of black, black, and more black, gave me a brief glance and a shrug, but she *almost* smiled. Apparently, our goth pansexual was in a good mood today.

"Welcome back, darling!" Raj said, flinging open their arms and grabbing me in a big hug.

I fell right into it and squeezed back as hard as I could, which made them let out a little yelp of surprise. I pulled back, and they frowned at me. "That bad?"

"I am *never* doing that without a phone ever again,"

I said. "I cannot survive my dad without you people."

"Aww, that's sweet." Raj pursed their lips in an over-the-top sad face. "And dramatic."

Lin smiled at them, then me, and rolled her eyes a little. Which reminded me.

"Did you know people think we're dating?" I said, poking Raj in one shoulder.

Raj's dark-brown eyes went wide. "*What*? They do?"

"Wait," Jessica said, and her usual affected 'I don't care' face *actually* frowned. "You two aren't dating?"

Raj and I both stared at her. Was this actually happening?

"You do everything together!" Jessica said, throwing up her hands.

"That's because he's my best friend," Raj said.

"I thought you were just being quiet about it," Lin said. "I figured you'd tell us when you were ready."

"You, too?" I faced Lin. Then I noticed Ethan and Grayson were being really quiet. I turned to Ethan. "Did you all think we were dating?"

They both looked uncomfortable.

I shook my head. "Wow." I looked at Raj. "I mean, no offence."

Raj laughed. "None taken. I adore you, mister. But I don't, like, *adore* you."

"Same." I gave them a fist bump.

"Sorry," Lin said, lifting her shoulder.

"It's okay," I said, then eyed the whole group. "But actually, there's something else that isn't okay."

That got their attention. I took a deep breath. I couldn't bring myself to say it while I was looking at Lin, so I faced Grayson and Ethan instead. Besides, they'd been the real instigators of this whole Team Lin, Team Jasmine stuff.

"We need to invite Jasmine and Roy to come with us to Prom," I said. "And we need to apologize to her." When Grayson opened his mouth, I held up my hand. "I'm not done," I said, remembering how when I'd done that to Caleb on the train, he'd stopped to listen.

Grayson didn't, though. "But — "

"I *said* I'm not done." I said it louder than anything

I'd ever said to anyone in the Rainbow Club before.

Grayson stopped talking. Everyone was staring at me now. *Be mad*, Caleb had said. Well, I was. At least a little. And some of it was at myself for not doing this last week.

"I get it might be awkward since you two broke up," I said, facing Lin for a second. She nodded, but she didn't seem mad or upset, so I went back to talking to the rest of the group. "But Jasmine is still part of the Rainbow Club. She's still queer. We rented the limo for the Rainbow Club and their dates. We can't drop her because she's dating a guy. That's gross. And really biphobic. And it means she should come," I said. I was starting to ramble a bit and tried to stop. "With Roy as her date."

Grayson stared at me, his eyes wide. He lifted one eyebrow like he was waiting for something.

"Oh, I'm done. That was it," I said, realizing I'd totally told him to shut up. My hands were shaking again. I thought maybe I might throw up. That *sucked*.

"I thought we agreed," Grayson said.

"No, you sort of *decided* and told the rest of us," Raj said. "Ben's right." Raj nodded at me. "She should come with us. They both should."

Grayson still looked a little mad, but this time, he didn't say anything. Predictably, Jessica looked bored more than anything else. She didn't really care about Prom at all. Ethan turned to Lin. "Lin?"

"Don't do that," Lin said, shaking her head. She sounded mad herself, now. "You've been doing that ever since we broke up. Don't make it *my* choice. That's not fair." Lin sighed. "But Ben's right. I never asked you to uninvite her." She took a breath. "And I shouldn't have let you. It was petty."

"You're allowed to feel bad, Lin," Raj said, stroking her arm.

"Okay," Ethan said, nodding. "I'll let Jasmine know." He smiled. "I'm glad."

"Hooray," Jessica said flatly, twirling one finger in the air. "Prom is saved." She rolled her eyes.

I looked at Lin. She gave me a nod. Okay. She wasn't mad at me. Or betrayed. Or whatever. I finally exhaled.

Ethan already had his phone out and was tapping away on it. Grayson was watching him.

"So," Raj said, dropping their voice a little to keep it just between us. "That was new for you. Very cool."

"You mean making waves?" I asked. "Thanks. I hated it."

Raj laughed, and I grinned at them. Then I noticed Caleb Khoury had arrived. He was at the other end of the hall, opening his locker, and chatting with a couple of his friends on the basketball team, Scott and Roy. At least Donovan wasn't there. Caleb pulled off his jacket, hanging it up, and once again I was treated to the sight of Caleb Khoury's arms, which were covered in a long-sleeved red shirt that seemed almost shrink-wrapped to his skin.

He looked *great*. I remembered the photos on his feed and had no trouble whatsoever imagining him taking the shirt off and diving into his pool. Then my imagination wondered what it might feel like to touch his skin when he was all warm from the sun and wet from the pool . . .

"Hello, Earth to Ben," Raj said.

"Sorry," I said, looking back at Raj. I could feel my face turning red. "What?"

"Welcome back," Raj said, laughing. "What was so fascinating?" They looked past me at the hallway for a few seconds before turning back to me.

"I'm trying to decide something," I said, glancing at Caleb again. Ugh. Why did he have to look so *good* all the time?

"Okay," Raj said. "Decide what?"

"I'm thinking of doing something really, really scary, and it could go *so* wrong," I said. "Like, spectacularly wrong. And publicly wrong, come to think of it. There are only a few weeks left of school. If it goes wrong, it would feel like forever. It would be *awful.* Which means I probably shouldn't do it, but — "

"Ben," Raj said, and though they had no idea what I was talking about, they grabbed my elbows and shook me to get my attention. "Are you overthinking it?"

"Of course, I am," I said. "Have you met me?"

Raj laughed. "It's up to you." It was such the

perfect Raj thing to say, but not actually helpful in the moment. I think they could tell, because they squeezed my elbows again, and said, "But if it's anything like what you just did with the Rainbow Club? I vote yes."

I laughed. "Way, *way* more scary."

"Then I definitely vote yes." Raj crossed their arms. "I like this version of you. Kind of badass."

"Badass?" I laughed at them. Oh, I was so not a badass. "Okay." I grinned and took their elbows and shook right back. "This is awful. I feel sick. You have to bury my body if I die."

"Deal," Raj said.

I turned and walked toward Caleb before I could change my mind.

15 Caleb Khoury Knows the Definition of Consequence

CALEB SAW ME COMING at the last moment, and he smiled, which helped. Or at least, I didn't throw up on the spot. But when I got there and opened my mouth, he started speaking before I could.

"The result or effect of an action or condition," he said carefully, and then smiled like he was proud of himself.

I blinked. "What?" Caleb's friends were staring at us, looking just as confused by whatever it was Caleb had just said.

"It's the definition of consequence," Caleb said. "You asked me if I knew what it was." He pulled something out of his locker and handed it to me.

I looked down. It was a phone protector. Bright red. When had he possibly had the time to get me a phone protector? Then I realized it wasn't brand new, but the case I'd seen on his phone on the train.

Was he giving me his phone protector?

"Is this yours?" I said, holding it up.

"It is. Was. It's a placeholder?" Caleb sounded flustered, and a little awkward. Was he nervous? "I wanted to get you one. I mean, I'm going to get you one." He smiled. "I'm sorry for breaking your phone." He lifted one eyebrow. "Was that a better apology?"

"Pretty much perfect," I said, gripping the phone case, and then . . . I did it. "Would you like to go out sometime?" The words almost came out normally. I only barely sounded like I was this close to passing out. I didn't dare look at his friends, because if they so much as grimaced, I'd die on the spot.

Caleb didn't grimace.

Caleb Khoury grinned. Full-on grinned. His dark-brown eyes flicked back and forth, and he was smiling at me like I'd made his day. Me. Ben Ross.

"Yeah," Caleb said. "I would. What do you want to do?"

Now his friends weren't possible to ignore. Scott shoved his shoulder, saying "Duuuude!" but in a teasing, friendly way. On the other side, Roy was watching us with this kind of stunned expression, but he eventually closed his mouth.

"I didn't get that far," I said, trying to ignore them and focus on the fact *Caleb freaking Khoury* wanted to go out on a date with me. "I figured we could do your thing. You know, make it up on the fly. Maybe we could watch *Spirited Away* so you can admit how wrong you are about how you ranked it."

"Don't make me change my mind, Benny," Caleb said, but the smile told me he was teasing.

"Fine, how about a prom threesome?" I said, because if he was going to tease me and call me Benny in front of his friends, I was happy to tease him right back.

Caleb burst out laughing. Both Scott and Roy looked completely floored. I shrugged at them.

"It's an inside joke," I said, because I was still me and there was no way I was letting them run away with that comment out of context. "I wasn't being serious."

"Okay," Scott said, laughing even louder.

"You," Caleb threw one of his incredible arms around my neck. "Are a menace, Benny Ross."

I didn't know what to do. He'd tugged me right up against him and there was nowhere for my hands to go. Also, my face felt like it was on fire. He grinned at me, and I'm sure my own expression was something close to stunned disbelief.

A second later, Roy said, "Incoming."

What? Incoming? I turned and saw Emma Tremblay heading toward us. Oh no. Tall, raven-haired, and put together perfectly in her skinny jeans and a burgundy sweater that I wouldn't have been surprised to learn was tailored personally for her, Emma didn't slow down one bit until she was face-to-face with Caleb.

I nearly pulled away, but when I looked at Caleb, he clenched his jaw. He loosened the arm he had wrapped around my neck but kept his hand on my shoulder. I followed his lead and stayed put.

Okay, fine. I froze in utter terror. Same thing.

"We need to talk," Emma said. She looked at me for a half-second, frowned at Caleb's hand on my shoulder, then dismissed me before aiming her blue eyes at Caleb. "In *private*," she said, crossing her arms.

Scott and Roy sort of took a few steps away, though they didn't go far enough to not be able to hear what was being said. Caleb didn't let me go, though, so I stayed put again.

Also, I didn't think my legs would work.

"Look," Caleb said. "I get you're mad about the car, but it's already taken."

"Caleb." Emma *pouted*. Like, she actually did the whole lip thing and tilted her head and made this little noise that sounded like someone had stepped on a mouse or something. "I called the rental place, and they don't have any more."

"Well, I'm using the one I paid for," Caleb said. "You already made it clear you didn't want to share it with anyone."

"What, you and Scott are going as *friends*?" Emma shook her head like she couldn't comprehend it, though I wasn't sure she wasn't also saying she thought Caleb and Scott were *more* than friends.

Maybe Emma was insecure?

"Yes," Caleb said. "We are. And I'm taking Benny as my date." He tugged me in a bit with his hand, which was good because otherwise, I would have fallen over on the spot.

I was his date for Prom? Since when?

Emma stared at me for what felt like forever. Then she looked at Caleb. Then me again.

"What?" she said. She didn't sound angry, just confused, and turned back to Caleb. "Is that a joke?"

Ouch.

"No. It's not. Benny asked me out," Caleb said.

"I said yes." I had no idea how Caleb was staring her down, but he was doing it. "I don't want this to be weird, Emma, and I'm sorry if it's hard for you. But I have a date for Prom, and I paid for the car." He let out a little sigh. "I'm sorry you're upset. But *you* broke up with me."

"And you're going with *Ben*?" she said. The way she said my name was not nice. "But you and Scott . . ."

"Okay, I'm *straight*," Scott said, and I'd lay odds it came out a lot louder than he intended because he sort of flinched. "Sorry. Nothing wrong with not being straight, obviously. But me and him is not a thing, Em."

"He's my best friend," Caleb said. "I don't want to sleep with him."

"But you do want to sleep with *Ben*?" She shook her head and held up her hands, gesturing at me like I was something she couldn't name.

Okay. I was dead. I had just died, and I was now a ghost. RIP me.

Also, I hated the way Emma Tremblay said my name.

"I'll probably kiss him first," Caleb said, shrugging.

"Wow," Emma said, and honestly, I couldn't read what she meant by the word. Like, was it 'wow, you moved on fast'? or 'wow, I could see you with Scott, but not with Ben'? I needed context here.

"Don't do that," Caleb said.

"Don't do what?" she said.

"Don't be mean to Benny," Caleb said. "You're mad at me, not him. Don't treat him like shit just because you're mad at me."

All right. Now I wanted to sleep with Caleb, too.

"Really?" she said. "You just drop that on me and that's it. I'm supposed to just accept that. And then you're all, 'Don't be mean to Ben.' *Wow*. I can't." She threw up both her hands, a look of total disgust on her face.

Then, to my complete surprise, she turned around and walked away.

She just *left*.

"Oh, thank God," Caleb said, letting out a huge breath of air. He glanced at me. "You okay?"

"We're going to Prom?" I said, turning to look at him. I also wanted more information on this whole him-wanting-to-kiss-me thing, but I didn't have the guts to ask in front of Scott and Roy.

"Sorry." Caleb cringed like he realized he sort of skipped the part where we'd agreed to do that. "But yes?" He leaned back. "If you want to?"

Did I want to go to Prom with Caleb Khoury? Was he kidding?

"Oh," I said. "I want to. Absolutely. Just maybe warn a guy. I don't like surprises, remember? Slow and steady on the rails. I'm the train."

"Does that mean I can't kiss you?" Caleb said. I could tell he was going for his smug smile, but it wobbled a bit, which was adorable, but did he just say what I thought he said? "Because I did mean that part."

"Oh my god, dude," Scott said, and it took me a second to realize Scott was talking to *me*, not Caleb. He had his hands together like he was begging me. "Please put him out of his misery. And mine. If I have to get one more midnight text about how he doesn't know how to make the first move with you because you're a dude — "

"Shut up!" Caleb said, shoving him, and laughing, and *blushing*. "Traitor!"

Caleb texted Scott about me? Last night? Holy crap.

"Caleb?" I said.

Caleb looked at me. One of his thick eyebrows rose.

I leaned forward and kissed Caleb, right there in the hallway, in front of his friends, and my friends — I *distinctly* heard Raj leading a cheer behind me — and then Caleb was kissing me back and I didn't hear much of anything after that. All I could process was how good a kisser he was and how he tasted like toothpaste and coffee.

Weird combo. But I didn't mind.

I pulled back first — because I was still me and a quick public kiss was one thing, but I wasn't going to make out in the hallway in front of everyone. Caleb grinned at me, and I was grinning back. I'd kissed *Caleb Khoury*. He was my freaking prom date.

Wait . . .

"You know what I just realized?" I said.

"What?" he said.

"If you're my prom date, then you don't need your car. The Rainbow Club has a limo and we're all going together with our dates." I smiled. "Including you and Jasmine, if you want," I said to Roy. "I'm sorry they were being so shitty to her. She should have gotten an apology by now, but you deserve one, too."

Roy gave me an odd look and nodded. "If she wants to."

Then I turned back to Caleb. "But this means you actually *could* give the car to Emma."

Caleb laughed. "Oh my God."

"She could go with Scott," I said, fighting back my own laugh. "As *friends*."

"Oh wow, seriously?" Scott said, looking at me with wide eyes. "I'm standing right here. You were right, Khoury. Benny is *brutal*."

"See?" Caleb said. He threw his arm around me again, and I put mine around his waist. It felt good there. I fit. My hands were barely shaking, even. Caleb winked at me, then looked back at Scott. "Don't get him mad at you. He holds a grudge."

"Oh, shut up," I said, and leaned in for another kiss. And this time? I didn't pull back.

ACKNOWLEDGEMENTS

I'd like to take a small moment to offer large thanks to everyone at Lorimer for making me feel so welcome, but most especially my editor, Allister, who fielded all my "so, how does this work here?" questions and always had answers. Editors are the unsung rock stars of the book world (and he's also a literal rock star, for the record). Major thanks also to all the teens who put up with my questions. I'm sorry your parents have such tragically uncool friends like me, but on the plus side, there's probably a character named after you in here somewhere. Lastly, but never least, thank you to my husband, Dan, who consistently cheers me on when I'm staring at the computer, convinced I'll never write another word, and also Max the Husky, who is a good dog enough of the time to get by. Those two keep me (relatively) on track. Sorry. I tried to resist a train pun, but it went off the rails.